MW01228113

AUTHOR'S NOTE

Seascapes and Vegas Mistakes contains a short prequel titled The Meeting which features the day *before* Isabel's return to Carolina Cove. Feel free to skip forward if you've already read.

THE MEETING—A SEASCAPES AND VEGAS
MISTAKES PREQUEL By Kay Lyons Copyright © 2022 by
Dorma Kay Lyons

All rights reserved.

No part of this book may be reproduced in any form or by any
electronic or mechanical means, including information storage
and retrieval systems, without written permission from the
author, except for the use of brief quotations in a book review.

THE MEETING–A SEASCAPES AND VEGAS MISTAKES PREQUEL

THE MEETING

BONUS CONTENT

I sabel Shipley smiled at the client who now walked away with the gallery manager to finish up the purchase details and smoothed a hand down her gold sequined cocktail dress. Her feet were killing her in the six-inch stilettos she wore, but she'd decided some Vegas glam was definitely in order when it came to her gallery showcase. The last-minute invitation might have been insulting to some, but she'd decided to look at it as an opportunity. That's why she'd scrambled to pack and ship her work and now stood inside of one of Vegas's vast hotels greeting locals and visitors alike.

"That looked like a promising transaction."

She turned at the sound of the deep voice and sucked in a quick breath. She'd noticed the man immediately when he'd wandered through the gallery doors, and in the last hour he'd made the rounds, lingering in her section and focusing on her paintings as though they were great works of art. She'd kept an eye on him as he'd studied her paintings, her mind whirling with the need to memorize his lean lines and angles for later, when she was home and able to create. "I believe so."

"Your work is amazing, Ms. Shipley."

Heat flooded into her face, and she blamed the hot spotlights shining down from above, even though they were focused on the art rather than the room. "Thank you. Please, call me Isabel," she said, holding out her hand.

"Everett Drake. Nice to meet you, Isabel. Michael said you were talented but I wasn't sure what to expect."

"Michael?"

"Devoncourt."

"You know my cousin?" she asked.

Everett nodded and held her hand longer than necessary, and she enjoyed the tingle of his touch racing up her arm. Like, seriously, was he for real?

"We're associates. Michael knew I'd be in Vegas this weekend and mentioned you'd be here and why. I'm glad I decided to check it out."

"Me, too. That's so sweet. I...I was told the last night is usually slow, so a friendly face is most welcome."

Oh, was he ever. The man was gorgeous. Tall, dark-haired with just a smattering of gray peeking through at his temples when he turned his head. He wore a dark charcoal suit that appeared tailor-made to fit his body.

"Things look to be wrapping up. I don't suppose you would like to join me for a celebration drink after you're finished here?"

She bit back a girlish *squee* and forced herself to keep her cool. After all, if Michael knew him and told Everett to check her out, well, that alone labeled him as safe. "I'd like that."

"Great. There's a bar next door. I'll wait for you there."

"Okay." Isabel watched him walk away, feeling more than a little wide-eyed at what had just transpired. She fought the urge to fan her face and was glad she hadn't lifted her hand when Everett glanced back at one last time before leaving the gallery, his gaze sliding over her like she wasn't the only one doing some memorizing.

She spent another twenty minutes talking to the gallery curator and saying goodbye to the friend who'd thought to include her when they'd had a cancellation. The remaining paintings would be packed and shipped once the display date was over and sales finalized.

That done, she'd grabbed her bag and ran into the gallery bathroom to freshen her makeup and took a fortifying breath before walking over to where Everett Drake waited.

He stood the moment he caught sight of her and welcomed her to the table by holding her chair while she settled.

"Are you hungry?" he asked. "I'll treat you to a celebratory dinner."

"No, not really. But, please, feel free to get something if you like."

He smiled at her and she found herself returning the grin.

"I'm fine. Champagne?"

"Oh, yes, please."

He lifted a hand and the waiter immediately appeared with a bottle of Dom. They really were going to celebrate.

She jumped when the waiter popped the cork and flushed when Everett chuckled softly at her response.

The waiter poured two glasses, and once the waiter left, Everett lifted his glass and held it while she matched his movements.

"To your talent and success."

"To new friends," she added.

Everett tipped his head in response to her toast, their gazes locked as they each sipped.

"So, tell me about Isabel."

Even though there was no reason to blush she felt the heat scalding her face. There was just something about him. "I'm an artist," she said, smiling when he did.

"Tell me something no one else knows."

The husky timbre of his voice left shivers racing over her skin. "I'm...not sure how to answer that. I don't think I know you well enough yet to share those kinds of secrets."

He grinned and dipped his head as though acknowledging her point and poured them another glass.

"What about you? Any secrets you'd like to share?" she asked.

"I've never been to Vegas before."

Oh! Same. Have you gone to any shows? Toured the casinos?"

The next hour was spent drinking the Dom and exchanging stories about miscellaneous things. She discovered Everett was in Vegas to attend his father's wedding, though the news didn't seem to be something he celebrated. Everett also admitted to a secret addiction to old eighties movies from the Gen X era and that led to a debate over the best movie ever.

"You'll never top Princess Bride."

"Hmm. I think I can," she said.

"With?"

"Can't Buy Me Love."

"Ahh, that is a good one," he said with an agreeable nod.

"Patrick Dempsey in his glorious nerdom and pre-heartthrob days."

Once the Dom was gone, Everett leaned forward

and brushed his fingertips over her cheek, smoothing her hair away from her face. She noticed his gaze lower and couldn't keep from wetting her lips. His eyes darkened and another shiver shot through her.

"Have you gambled while you've been here?" he asked, changing the subject.

She bit her lower lip and shook her head. "I haven't really had time. And I leave tomorrow so... There answer is no."

He moved his hand into his jacket pocket and removed his wallet, pulling out several bills to pay the tab and tip generously. "There's no time to waste then," Everett said as he got to his feet and held out a hand for her. "What's your pleasure?"

She hadn't spent so much as a quarter in a slot machine so after they left Everett escorted her to an empty one. They played a few rounds, laughing all the while at some of the characters camped out in front of the other machines. From there they tried their hand at blackjack and Izzy was well aware of the admiring looks Everett received from female passersby. Everett had that classic kind of handsome-ness found in old black and white movies, the ones where angled jawlines, tailored suits, and quippy damsels in distress were a thing.

After losing several hands to the house, they moved on to roulette.

"Winner gets a kiss," Everett murmured into her ear as he placed several chips on black.

Maybe it was the champagne slowly fading from her system or the geeky side of Everett that loved old movies, or the fact he seemed just a bit sad and she wanted to make him laugh and remember their Vegas adventure fondly. Whatever it was, she bit her lip and stared up at him as she placed her bet on red.

"Your prize?" he asked.

She pondered the question for a long moment. "If I win, we go to one of those fake wedding chapels to get married and send Michael the photos for a prank," she said, the words leaving her in a gush because she couldn't believe she had the audacity to propose marriage—even a fake one—to someone she barely knew. "He's always pulling pranks with me and my cousins and it's about time I freak him out, if only a little."

Everett's rumbling laugh and gorgeous smile filled her stomach with butterflies and the slow burn of something she couldn't allow herself to acknowledge for fear it wasn't reciprocated.

"Deal."

She shot him what she hoped was a flirtatious glance from beneath her lashes and placed her chips on red. Izzy bit her lower lip, watching as the attendant set the wheel in motion. She found herself holding her breath, hoping beyond hope for the night to get a whole lot more interesting.

Seconds later she gasped out a laugh and turned

to bask in her triumph. "Looks like we're goin' to the chapel," she said in a sing-song voice.

It took mere seconds to google the closest fake chapel and head in that direction.

They laughed and flirted on their way out of the casino and when a group of four men stumbled their way too close, Everett wrapped a protective arm around her shoulders and pulled her to his side, shielding her from their drunken revelry. Isabel leaned her head on Everett's shoulder, breathing in his tantalizing cologne and memorizing every detail of this day.

MAYBE IT WAS crazy and over the top, but it was her last night in Vegas and she was up for something fun and silly after a week of stress. Especially when it involved the gorgeous man beside her. What woman wouldn't want to fake marry a man like him? And she'd have pics to show for it. Something to remember this wonderful night where her career was finally looking up and she'd snagged the attention of Michael's gorgeous friend who made her pulse flutter and her knees weak.

They made their way through the crowd and down the street to the building, following the map's walking directions until they reached a set of doors. "Here comes the bride and groom," she said.

Everett's smile and the slight shake of his head

left her laughing, and she burst into the building the moment he opened the door.

It didn't take long. The chapel had the process down to a science, and within moments, she was tucked into a long white dress, handed silk flowers and a veil, and followed the attendant to the chapel area where Everett waited in a tuxedo that looked a size too small for his tall frame.

The officiant looked like a former Elvis impersonator, but as the photographer clicked away, they took their vows and Everett slid a gaudy, cheesy double-dice ring on her finger before he tugged her close for their wedding kiss. A kiss that seemed to surprise him, too, if his heated expression was anything to go by when he lifted his head.

The second kiss was longer, deeper than the first, and she gasped for air and clarity when the officiant cleared his throat and mentioned others were waiting.

They quickly changed back into their street clothes and gathered the photos and fake marriage certificate from the receptionist. Standing in a corner of the busy lobby, Izzy took a pic of their photo and texted it to Michael.

Mr. and Mrs.!
What???
We got married! When in Vegas...
SERIOUSLY?

Yup. Everett is a great guy! We just decided to go for it. Why not?

Everett's phone buzzed and he removed it from his pocket and chuckled when he saw Michael's name.

They kept the game up for several minutes until Izzy pushed it too far when she said she and Everett were honeymooning in Morocco. Michael messaged back that he knew better since he had an upcoming meeting with Everett that the man wouldn't dare miss and their prank unraveled from there.

Laughing at their fun and Michael's admission that they'd pranked him, Everett tugged her out the door of the chapel and they returned to the hotel where it had all started. Everett kissed her on the elevator and then walked her back to her room, his arm around her shoulders even though this time there were no drunken strangers making it necessary.

"That was fun," she said outside her room. "Now when we play Never Have I Ever, we can say we've been married in Vegas."

Everett chuckled at her words, and as always, a thrill coursed through her. She liked his deep, rumbling laugh, even though it had sounded a bit rusty at the beginning of the night.

She passed the keycard over the black face above the knob and opened the door to stash her purse and the oversized envelope with their photos and certificate on the hall table. Everett blocked the door and kept it from closing, watching, and she could feel the heat of his gaze on her skin. "It was really nice to meet you, Everett. You made my last night in Vegas the best."

"I feel the same."

She wished she had more nerve, enough to-- "So, um, I have an early flight. I should…"

She watched as Everett's gaze lowered to her lips, and she instinctively flicked her tongue to wet them. A good-night kiss from him would not be a bad thing.

She heard his low groan, the breath leaving her lungs in response as he stepped forward and let the door shut behind him. He gently prodded her back against the wall and lowered his head, pressing his lips to hers.

That kiss…

Everett stole her senses, her mind. Her body. She wrapped her arms around his neck and reveled in the embrace as one kiss blended into many, many more. It was the goodbye she didn't want on a night she didn't want to end.

But her flight left first thing in the morning and she didn't do things like this. Meet men in bars and--

"Isabel…"

Her name was a low growl filled with every ounce of desire and awareness she felt in response to his touch, and she understood the silent question. "Don't go," she heard herself whisper, lifting onto her toes to kiss him again so she could close her eyes and pretend all would be fine in the morning even though she knew she'd leave a part of her heart behind.

Everett raised his head and avoided her kiss and when she felt his fingers gently grasp her chin she forced her lashes up. Stared into his gaze as he searched hers.

That low rumbling growl mixed with a groan made her toes curl. And then he kissed her again.

Biiiiig surprises are in store for Isabel and Everett. Turn the page to keep reading Seascapes and Vegas Mistakes.

SEASCAPES AND VEGAS MISTAKES

A CAROLINA COVE NOVEL

KAY LYONS

KINDRED SPIRITS PUBLISHING

SEASCAPES AND VEGAS MISTAKES by Kay Lyons

Copyright © 2022 by Dorma Kay Lyons

978-1-953375-21-6

978-1-953375-22-3

All rights reserved.

This is a work of fiction. Names, characters, places, and incidents are the product of the author's imagination and are used fictitiously. Any resemblances to actual events, locales, or persons living or dead, is purely coincidental.

No part of this book may be reproduced in any form or by any electronic or mechanical means, including information storage and retrieval systems, without written permission from the author, except for the use of brief quotations in a book review.

SEASCAPES AND VEGAS MISTAKES

CHAPTER ONE

"Hey, I can tell you're exhausted from your week in Vegas but what's up with you?" Amelia asked, sliding Izzy a searching glance from the driver's seat. "I thought you'd be bouncing off the walls with excitement."

Isabel Shipley—Izzy to her friends and family—lifted a hand to rub her upper chest and wondered if it was time to break down and take something for the anxiety plaguing her ever since waking up in her hotel room this morning on her last day in Las Vegas.

The rumpled bed had said a lot of things, but it was the running shower and suddenly pounding head that wouldn't allow her to put two and two together and come up with anything other than sheer panic. Especially when a glance at the bedside clock gave her barely an hour to get to the airport and through Vegas security for her flight back home to Carolina Cove, North Carolina.

Given her frantic state to get out while the gettin' was good, she'd scrambled into clothes she'd purposely left out because she *always* ran late and grabbed the suitcase she had haphazardly packed the day before on a break from the gallery. After a last horrified glance at the open bathroom door and the scrumptiousness she left behind, she'd made a run for the hills and hopefully the return of her sanity.

She didn't *do* things like this. Ever.

So why had she?

Adrenaline had given her just enough mindfulness to hail a taxi, but the TSA line was long and she'd had to freaking *run* for her gate, arriving mere seconds before the door to the plane shut behind her as the last one to board.

Head throbbing from the stress ice pick stabbing her brain, she'd curled up against the window, her mind racing with questions and embarrassment as memories of the previous night surfaced until she fell into a fitful doze that came from too much stress, not enough sleep, a physical soreness that brought a blush to her cheeks.

Hours after leaving the hotel room and Vegas behind, her mind still hadn't come up with any logical answers. Truthfully, she couldn't even blame the champagne she'd drunk.

She'd only had three glasses over a span of time, but her excitement and adrenaline had known no bounds. And what better way to celebrate the completion of her first *real* showcase than with a tall, dark, and very gorgeous man?

He'd made her tingle. Like, seriously, *tingle*. She hadn't known such a thing was possible. Even more amazing, he'd seemed genuinely interested in her art and process, which was *such* a turn-on itself.

He also knew her cousin Michael and had attended her showcase because of it –which made him safer than the average Joe.

"Izzy? Seriously, you're worrying me. What's up?" her best friend asked.

Izzy watched as Amelia ran a hand over her rapidly expanding belly in a soothing-mama gesture and swallowed hard. She had to snap out of it. If anyone should be freaking out, it was Amelia. She was the one with twins on the way.

Izzy nodded to herself. *Suck it up, buttercup.* What was done was done. She and Everett had flirted, sipped luscious champagne, played blackjack and...made a bet. Which was how she'd wound up listening to the shower spray in the next room.

Winner gets a kiss, he'd said.

Loser has to— "I-I...I'm fine. Just really, *really* tired." Because while her challenge hadn't been anything outrageous, it *had* led to the aftermath.

"But your show was a success? You texted and said you'd scored some good commissions and would text me later to tell me details."

Thankful for the distraction, Izzy turned her attention to the passing scenery. "Yeah, sorry about that. I went to the bar for a drink and...talked to friends."

Friend, rather. That's where she'd met him again. The handsome not-so-stranger who'd wandered through the gallery around each of her paintings as though looking over a Monet or something equally amazing. Everett had introduced himself as a long-time friend of her cousin Michael's, said that he'd seen her name on the signs about the gallery show, and remembered Michael bragging about his talented artist cousin and the timing of her upcoming show.

They'd chatted briefly, her entire body humming with excitement because he was so...*so fine.*

But it wasn't until later when she'd met up with him in the bar that things had gone from casual conversation to major flirtation.

"I thought as much. You know, sometimes it really comes down to the people you know, which is why it's so important to get out there. So? Tell me. Who bought your work? Anyone famous?"

Izzy frowned. She'd stayed so busy in Las Vegas prepping for the show after the last-minute inclusion that she hadn't had time to miss home. But now that she was here?

The familiar sights and traffic signs pointing to Carolina Cove brought tears to her eyes and comfort to her soul.

Or maybe it was the relief that she could almost shut herself inside her apartment and pretend the last twelve hours hadn't happened?

Or relive them.

To be honest, it was a toss-up as to which she'd prefer.

How could a thirty-two-year-old woman get herself into such a pickle?

God forbid she ever admit this, but maybe her mother was right? She was too old for this. The games that came with dating and...

It's not dating when it's a one-night stand.

Which she didn't do.

Ever.

Except with someone Michael knows?

Her cousin wasn't a saint by any means, but she was pretty sure he wouldn't want to go to a business meeting and find out what had happened to his "kid cousin" in Vegas. And if memory served, Michael and Everett were currently working on a project.

Great. Oh, great.

"Iz?"

She had to really focus to remember Amelia's question. "Um, I-I don't know. The buyers finalized everything with the curator. I'll get more details this week, I'm sure. There...wasn't much time there at the end." Because she'd finished the show floating on a cloud, having made plans to meet Everett to celebrate the completion.

"Well, it's fantastic. I'm so proud of you," Amelia said, sliding Izzy another glance from across the way as she crossed the bridge toward Carolina Cove.

"Thanks. I mean, they could always change their mind but—"

"No buts. It's awesome and doubtful that would happen, so accept the sales as a win. I'm happy for you."

"Yeah. It's just...surreal." *In so many ways*.

She appreciated Amelia's support. Her friend was the best, softhearted and understanding and supportive even though Izzy's crazy ideas weren't always thought through.

"Okay, so, you're only minutes away from home. Take today off to recoup and rest, and then you can hit the ground running tomorrow."

"Yeah, I think I might." Sleep was good. It would bring clarity. Right? Maybe then she could figure out exactly how she'd gone from being a not-so-wild child to waking up with a virtual stranger.

She'd had boyfriends. Two long-term ones and a handful of wannabes. But despite what people—especially her mother—might believe about artists and her so-called bohemian lifestyle, she wasn't a casual hookup kind of girl.

And other than talking and laughing and kissing —a *lot*—she wasn't sure when the scales had tipped during the night. Only that she'd allowed Everett to walk her to her hotel room in the wee hours of the morning after all their fun—and then invited him inside.

"Thanks again for picking me up."

"Absolutely. The timing couldn't have worked out better. I can drop you off and head to the film location to look around and still make it home early. I want to do something special for Lincoln's birthday. Especially since this is our last birthday alone for a while."

Izzy watched as Amelia slid her hand over her pregnant belly again and loved how happy her friend seemed to be. Pregnancy definitely agreed with her. "Good thing I have my sunglasses on," she teased. "You're absolutely glowing."

Amelia laughed, her earrings brushing her shoulders as she shrugged.

"I feel like it. I mean, it's weird but I have all of this *energy*. I'm told it's not the norm and usually the opposite is true, but I think I could climb mountains with energy to spare."

Izzy thought of how tired her older sister, Allie, had been during her pregnancies and shook her head. Definitely not the norm. "Just don't overdo it,"

Izzy said, wishing she could borrow some of that energy right now. Maybe then she wouldn't feel as though she'd been dragged out to sea by a riptide and been swimming against the current for days.

"Oh, I won't. I couldn't if I wanted to. Lincoln has been waiting on me hand and foot when I get home from work, and no one on set will let me lift a finger. Oh! Crap."

"What?"

"Well, before I forget...I ran into the Babes while you were gone."

"And?"

"I hate to say it, but your mom *insists* we use her house for the baby shower you're hosting. I hope that's okay? When I told them we were going to have it downstairs at London's Lattes, the Babes...well, they made it *really* hard to say no."

No doubt they had. The Babes rarely took no for an answer to anything. But why should they when the five older women had been catered to their whole lives?

During the summers of '58 and '59, four prominent Carolina Cove neighbors and friends had given birth to baby girls. One even had a set of twins. The proud mothers had taken the babes for daily strolls in their prams—and the locals had nicknamed them the Boardwalk Babes—a name used to this day by the now sixty-somethings.

All in all, Izzy had four pseudo aunts and ten

"cousins," seven female and three male—with the twin Babes each having a set of twins of their own—ranging in age from mid-forties all the way down to Izzy's thirty-two. Growing up, it had sucked to always be the youngest. Even more so because not only had her two older sisters treated her like the baby but all of her "cousins" had as well. She'd always been the kid sister no one wanted tagging along to dampen their fun.

"Okay," Amelia said, turning down the street toward London's Lattes and pulling to a stop behind Izzy's VW Bug convertible. Betty the Bug might be old, but she was still just as pretty as the day Izzy had bought her. Minus a little sun damage the south was known for.

"Need help getting in?" Amelia asked.

"No. I've got it. Thanks."

Izzy had rented the apartment above the coffee shop a little over a year ago when London Cohen, owner of London's Lattes, had met and then married a northern transplant who'd moved to the beach with his adopted children. Making rent wasn't always easy with her sporadic sales, but there was no denying being on her own gave Izzy a sense of freedom and independence she'd longed for after far too many years under her parents' roof.

Living a minimalist lifestyle made it easier to live sale to sale, but it didn't leave much in the bank after-wards. Not that her parents needed to know that.

But thankfully with her commissions from the Vegas showcase, she now had a cushion that would allow her to breathe for at least six months. She would put that time to good use.

Her mother had never understood why Izzy felt the need to move out of their garage apartment into an apartment several blocks away, but Izzy knew if she ever had a hope of proving her abilities and worth, she had to stand on her own. Even if it meant giving up more than a few luxuries. Life was about more than just things. It was experiences and moments...moments she captured and painted because she couldn't imagine doing anything else with her life—no matter what her family said.

"Okay, so get in there and get some rest. You don't seem like yourself, and you'll need all the energy you can muster now that the Babes are involved in the baby shower. I have a feeling things might be a little over-the-top now."

"Ain't that the truth," Izzy muttered, pulling her lips into a wry twist of dread. If her mother and the rest of the Babes knew one thing, it was how to entertain. Nothing could be simple. A party—especially a baby shower welcoming a new life into the world—would be "Babe-ified" in the extreme.

"Sorry. I know I should've protested more, but you know how they can be."

"Trust me, I know," Izzy said truthfully. "And it's not a problem. I'm used to dealing with my mother and the Babes. No worries." While navigating the Babes might make shower prepping more stressful, Izzy wouldn't be responsible for footing the bill on the Babes' many additions to the planning. If nothing else, that was a win for her in a time when she needed to bank and save as much as she could for a rainy day.

"Iz?"

Izzy was halfway out the door when Amelia stopped her. "Yeah?"

"What's with the ring? You're pretty eclectic but that's not exactly your usual style," Amelia said with a wry expression and a little laugh.

Izzy glanced down at the gaudy, sparkling double dice ring she wore on the ring finger of her left hand. One she'd thought about taking off on the plane but hadn't because of the memories it now held in the somewhat sensual-coated space in her brain from last night.

The fun of three glasses of bubbly seemed like a good idea while she had such a great time with a handsome, charismatic man. "Oh, it's just, um, a souvenir," she said, swallowing hard because of the way her heart began to pound in her chest when an image appeared in her mind. The champagne-coated edges of her memories sharpened, and she zeroed in on the moment her gorgeous companion had slid the ring onto her finger, a smile on his seductive lips that she'd matched with one of her own.

"Good thing. For a second there I thought you'd gone and gotten married in Vegas."

Izzy released a laugh that sounded shriller than she'd intended and slid her purse to her shoulder. "You know how it goes. What happens in Vegas stays in Vegas."

CHAPTER TWO

Everett Drake glanced at his watch for the nth time, his impatience growing with every second spent on the private jet. It had been five long, work-filled days since he'd opened his eyes Sunday morning in the Vegas suite beside Isabel, and he couldn't wait to see her again.

He'd left the bed long enough to shower, but when he'd returned, Isabel was nowhere to be found. Her purse and suitcase were gone, the clothes he'd seen draped over the chair missing as well. Without so much as a note on the nightstand or a *thank you, sir*.

His college buddy's cousin had since ignored his numerous attempts to contact her, which yet another reason to travel south. He wasn't used to being dismissed so casually, nor was he used to a woman walking away the way Isabel had.

Following her immediately hadn't been an option due to a series of prescheduled business meetings that required his presence in New York City, but now the wait was over, and he found himself chasing the thrill of Isabel as much as he had been that night.

The moment the jet touched down on the tarmac, Everett headed toward the door, followed by his personal assistant, Jacob, and Tomas, a bodyguard contracted from Guardian Group who also acted as his driver.

Jacob was a worrier and had managed to convince Everett that *this time* he really needed to bring Tomas along on the trip. No doubt Jacob felt two pairs of eyes on him were better than none and might keep him out of trouble.

"Sir?"

Everett had paused at the top of the stairs leading to the waiting SUV below. All to take in the sun where it hung low in the sky, promising a sunset full of spectacular cotton-candy-like pastels.

Everett glanced over his shoulder in time to catch Jacob's look of surprise that his billionaire boss had paused long enough to partake in something as uneventful as the sky. Apparently this was the week for surprises.

In the time since his father's wedding in Vegas to wife number eight, Everett had had plenty of opportunity to think about things. That's what brought him to Carolina Cove.

That and Isabel. Her cooperation would be key, after all.

Luggage transferred, the three of them made their way to the SUV for the drive to Carolina Cove. Jacob had arranged for an oceanfront rental located a few blocks from Isabel's tiny apartment above a coffeehouse, and Everett hoped the convenience to her would make things easier during his stay. They had details to discuss. A lot of them.

Forty-five minutes after landing, Tomas crossed the bridge leading to Carolina Cove.

The traffic heading out of Wilmington had been bumper-to-bumper, allowing time for several phone calls and meetings to be conducted. He'd never been to Wilmington before, but he'd heard about the city's rapid growth and movie industry from Isabel, her cousin, and Tomas, who'd interviewed in Wilmington with Guardian Group before being sent to New York for work.

"Mr. Drake? Michael Devoncourt for you."

Everett accepted the cell from Jacob and pressed it to his ear. "Michael."

"Did I hear correctly? Our meeting has been relocated to Carolina Cove? You're in town?"

"Just made it to the island."

"I don't believe it. Everett Drake is actually taking a vacation?"

"You've invited me to visit often enough. I thought I'd finally take you up on it."

Everett chatted with Michael a few minutes longer regarding the upcoming meeting and hung up just as Tomas pulled into a driveway and parked.

Everett exited the vehicle and turned to take in the home and the neighborhood fronting the Atlantic.

The three-story dwellings were a variety of shapes, sizes, and colors, but all blocked the sun setting behind them, casting a shadow over the dunes and halfway across the sand.

Pelicans swooped down and skimmed the surface of the Atlantic with agile grace, and in the distance, the pier was lined with fishermen and tourists alike.

From the look of things, Carolina Cove was a far cry from the Hamptons or Martha's Vineyard, but he had to admit the seaside town had its own charm. Despite the dinner-hour traffic and busy boardwalk, the area was relatively quiet and tranquil. So unlike the rush, crush, and busyness that was everything New York City.

Maybe it was because of all the stories Michael and Isabel had told him of this place and the people here. That or the long days and sleepless nights spent working in order to travel to Isabel in person had finally caught up with him and made him nostalgic for the sense of community and roots he'd never really had.

Inside the home, Everett took a quick tour before changing out of his suit into comfortable, casual clothes. Jacob had checked the weather reports before boarding, and Everett's housekeeper had packed an assortment of clothing to accommodate the warmth of the November days as well as the evening chill. Jacob had arranged grocery delivery through the booking agency, so the house was well stocked.

Everett left the two grumbling men behind, determined to see Isabel alone. He didn't feel the need to have a shadow for the short walk to Isabel's apartment, and he certainly didn't want to have to explain Tomas's presence when he lurked in the shadows like a ghost.

In shorts and a lightweight pullover and sporting sunglasses to combat the day's last blinding rays as he headed west, he knew he had the appearance of just another tourist visiting the area.

Everett hoped the time alone on the walk would help him gather his thoughts for how to broach the conversation to come, but his mind whirled as he analyzed his proposal all over again.

Who was Isabel Shipley? Was she really as intriguing as he'd found her in Vegas?

Everett walked the few blocks to the coffee shop beneath Isabel's apartment and stepped inside, suddenly in need of a few more minutes to put his thoughts in order.

The woman behind the counter smiled as he entered.

"Welcome to London's Lattes. What can I get for you?"

He placed an order for two and distracted himself by studying the various items on display and for sale.

"Just visiting or a new resident?" the woman asked as she worked.

Everett glanced around and realized she spoke to him. "Uh, visiting. Any recommendations? I landed about an hour ago."

A small smile pulled at the woman's mouth as she nodded.

"Well, you're off to a good start," she said, setting one cup on the counter. "Best coffee around. Other than that, be sure to check out the pier, pier house and aquarium, and downtown Wilmington. There's a lot of history here if that's your sort of thing. Especially if you like pirates."

"Pirates?"

"Mmm. Blackbeard, Stede Bonnet... Oh, and there's the battleship *North Carolina* docked across the river as well. You could also do a day trip to Bald Head Island or Southport. There's no shortage of things to do here. It's just a matter of preference."

"I'll check them out. Thanks." He tucked the

information back for reference later, hoping to explore the area with Isabel at his side. Maybe that would help break the tension he instinctively knew would be present?

He'd always been a sucker for historical facts, and growing up, he'd dreamed of actually being a pirate king. The memory brought a rare smile to his lips. He couldn't have been more than four or five at the time, racing through the house while wearing his eye patch and hat and carrying a tiny plastic sword.

The memory following it, however, was not as pleasant.

"Here's your order. Can I get you anything else?"

Drawn back to the present, he remembered Isabel's penchant for chocolate desserts and added two chocolate-drizzled scones to the order. While the barista bagged those, he pulled out his card to pay.

The woman lifted a delicate eyebrow high at the sight of the black card but didn't say anything as he swiped it and added a generous tip. "Thanks for the info," he said.

"Any time. Come back again soon."

He lifted the bag and coffee carrier and quickly left the coffee shop only to pause along the sidewalk entrance to the apartment upstairs.

He stared up at the second-floor window. *You've secured billion-dollar deals. You can handle one tiny woman.*

But could he?

What would it be like seeing her again? Would he feel the same instant pull to Isabel as he had in Vegas? Chemistry so strong he hadn't been able to keep himself from touching her? Or had it been the dim lights, their celebration of her show, not to mention his own melancholy at the time, combined with Isabel's bright, smiling persona that had charmed him into thinking it was more than a hookup?

Everett inhaled before opening the outer door. The interior held a musty yet coffee-and-chocolate-tinged scent.

The stairs squeaked as he made his way up them to a hallway and the single door at the end, and once again he paused to collect himself.

In the days since leaving Las Vegas, he'd had a background check performed on Isabel. That's how he knew about the apartment and her family, and he now had a better understanding of her relationship with Michael Devoncourt. They weren't blood-related cousins but merely the children of best friends, a group whose connections dated back long before Isabel and Michael were born.

He couldn't imagine having a family that size, even an extended one. Though he supposed his father's seven wives and their children would count as his extended family if one chose to think of them that way. He didn't...but only because he'd never had much contact with any of them.

Everett knocked softly and waited. And waited.

Knocking again received the same response, and after choking down his disappointment because not a single sound could be heard on the other side, he retraced his steps.

The barista who'd filled his coffee order was walking down the sidewalk toward the back of the building with a bag of trash and saw him exiting the apartment entrance.

"Oh. Hello again," she said, her expression full of curiosity. "Can I help you with something?"

Everett felt ridiculous, like a teenager hiding in the bushes to scope out his crush, and was thankful he'd left Isabel's coffee and scones outside her door. "No, thanks."

"Not home, huh?" she asked with a head tilt toward the door.

"I'll try again some other time." He'd hoped the evening hour meant catching Isabel at home so their conversation could remain private, but instead of planting himself on one of the outdoor benches or upstairs in the hallway and waiting for her like a stalker, he felt it best to move on. In the meantime, he'd drink his coffee and...maybe take a walk on the beach? Jacob and Tomas would not approve, but again, incognito had its benefits. No one would guess he'd be anywhere near Carolina Cove, much less out of New York City.

"You know, when Izzy stopped by yesterday, she said something about a baby shower for a friend at her parents' house. I believe it was this evening."

He tucked the information back with a nod. "Thanks. Maybe I'll stop by there."

"I could give her a message if you like," the woman said next. "Text her that you're coming so she can be on the lookout for you?"

"I appreciate that but I'm hoping to surprise her." He watched as the woman's gaze sparkled with unspoken questions.

"I see. Well, have a good evening," she murmured.

"Thanks. And thanks for the coffee. It's good."

The woman walked away with the trash while he turned on his heel and headed back toward the boardwalk and the ocean.

Once he reached the boardwalk, Everett paused long enough to pull up the recently acquired info on Isabel's family. He found her parents' address and lifted his head to get his bearings before he used his GPS and followed the boardwalk lining the dunes down several streets.

The views from the wooden planks were spectacular, and with the seagulls squawking overhead and the waves crashing against the shore, some of the tension inside him eased with every darkening shade of the sky.

He took off the sunglasses and shoved them into the V of his shirt for safekeeping, then stared up at the elegant house belonging to Adam and Mary Elizabeth Shipley.

Knocking would mean coming up with an excuse for him seeking Isabel out in such a manner. Something a man didn't do at this time of the evening without a very good reason. He had one. But not one he wanted to share among her family and friends just yet.

A child's laugh sounded from behind him and drew his immediate attention. He watched as a man, woman, and the little girl moved off the boardwalk and crossed to a house farther down the street, using the seaside entrance.

What would it have been like to grow up here? Summers spent playing with your neighbors and siblings? Days on the sand rather than a cold and sterile boys' school or at camp studying, training, or working? Evenings putting together puzzles or blowing bubbles or playing at the arcade he'd noted a few doors down from the pier?

The front door opened and a small group of women left the house. He nodded at them, catching the smiles and looks of interest as they passed him.

Instinct kicked in and Everett hustled up the steps, catching the door before it closed. Maybe it was presumptuous of him to simply enter, but given the crowd, he'd take his chances.

He paused just inside, noting the elegant furnishings and party decorations as well as the remaining well-dressed guests chatting in small groups as they gathered purses and jackets.

Laughter drew his attention, and he followed the sound into what appeared to be a living room. A balloon arch lined the wall of windows facing the ocean, and a mountain of gifts in baby-oriented bags were stacked in and around an empty chair.

Everett heard a familiar laugh and turned toward the left, zeroing in on Isabel's blond hair in the adjoining kitchen. She laughed again at something someone said, the sound throaty just as tempting as he remembered.

Silence descended the moment one of the women with Isabel spotted him. Several ladies now stared his way, and Isabel turned to see what had captured their attention and turned the chatty group silent.

"Hello. May we help you?" an older woman asked, giving him a wary glance.

He forced his attention away from Isabel and on to the woman. "Yes. Please, forgive the intrusion."

Isabel looked wide-eyed and completely shell-shocked as recognition dawned, and Everett questioned his timing once more. Maybe he should've waited to find her, but having spent the week unable to contact her, he hadn't wanted to wait another second. "I apologize for letting myself in, but the door was open and... I'm Everett Drake, a friend of Isabel's."

"Well, don't just stand there. Come in," another woman said, sliding Isabel a questioning glance.

When Isabel remained unmoving and mute, he chuckled and hoped she wouldn't come to and make a scene before he could explain himself. "Surprise."

Isabel's throat moved as she swallowed hard, her hand fluttering in front of her. In the other, she held a small plate of finger food.

"Isabel?" the older woman said.

Isabel finally straightened to her full height and set the plate aside, moving quickly to where he stood. "Everett," she said, greeting him with a strained smile.

He didn't allow the forced cheerfulness to bother him. He imagined she was quite surprised to see him.

Whispering for his ears only under the guise of a hug, she asked, "What are you *doing* here?"

His gaze swept over the many feminine faces watching their every move before he lowered his lashes and planted a chaste kiss on her cheek to disguise his murmur. "We need to talk."

"About?"

"The fact that we're legally married, *wife*."

CHAPTER THREE

Izzy wanted the ground to open up and swallow her. She'd go willingly, like a human sacrifice. Toss herself into the volcano and sing on the way down if that's what it took to get this moment to be a bad dream.

Anything to get away from the stares of the Babes, Amelia, and her sister-in-law, as well as local celeb and professional matchmaker Marsali Jones, all of whom watched her like hawks.

Her sisters had also lingered behind to pitch in for baby shower cleanup and entered the room from wherever they'd been chatting with the last of the guests, but now the combined stares left Isabel wishing Everett had timed his arrival to...well, never.

Had he said *wife?*

"Isabel, is everything all right?" her mama asked

in an obvious attempt to get their handsome guest to repeat his whispered words louder for their benefit.

Isabel felt the heat of embarrassment rolling off her in sweaty, unladylike waves and wondered if her mother and the rest of those watching could see her mortification.

She didn't know how, didn't know why, but what had happened in Vegas had *not* stayed in Vegas and now stood in front of her in all six feet four inches of sexiness with a stare that made her knees weak even now—despite the bomb he'd just dropped.

Had he really said wife?

"Iz?" Amelia murmured, snapping Isabel out of the fear-laced fog shrouding her.

"Isabel, where are your manners?" her mother said.

"Yeah, sis, introduce us," Allie urged.

Knowing she had to get her act together fast, Isabel made the mistake of meeting Allie's gaze and found her eldest sister's shrewd eyes narrowed on her with all the *caught-you* knowingness a sibling could possess.

Isabel's chest squeezed with the inability to breathe properly, and she actually seemed to have a small panic attack—because wouldn't that just be the thing to happen next? Anxiety sucked and panic attacks were from the devil himself, but right now?

It might get her out of the room.

Not for the first time, Izzy regretted tattling on

Allie so many times as a kid. Maybe if she hadn't, Allie would've run interference instead of adding to the chaos currently making her entire body sweat like an MMA fighter. "Um, yeah. Of course. This is, um, Everett."

Did her voice have to sound so...husky?

The night with Everett presented itself in adrenaline-fueled, detailed memories and images, but one thing was for certain, the marriage *wasn't* real. She couldn't have messed up that much. Could she?

They.

They couldn't have messed up that badly. Because he had been there, too. All seventy-six inches of him. "Everett, th-this is my mother, Mary Elizabeth, my aunts Tessa, Cheryl, Adaline, and Rayna Jo. Best friend and mommy-to-be, Amelia, her sister-in-law, Marsali, and my sisters, Allie and Sophia."

The gorgeous man next to her chuckled softly and accepted her mother's outstretched hand, shaking it gently.

"Ladies. I thought my timing was off, but I can see now that it was perfect," Everett said, smiling at the group ogling him like a sweet treat.

"It's wonderful to meet you," her mama said, the sentiment echoed by the other Babes, who smiled *waaay* too widely.

It was true that the man was as handsome as they came, not to mention charming, and obviously not a bum sleeping on the beach as part of his attempt to find himself.

You were twenty...and into musicians. You've grown up since then.

But in a fit of anger, her twenty-year-old self had still brought the beach bum to meet her parents and had paid him to sit through a torturous dinner after they'd attempted to set her up with someone they approved of—even though that someone had date raped a girl she'd known in high school. It just proved how no one really knew anyone. Not really. Lots of things happened behind closed doors that no one talked about.

"Likewise."

Once the Babes finished making a fuss over him and more handshakes were completed, an awkward silence settled over the room.

"Uh, Everett, Isabel didn't mention you'd be visiting us," her mother said, giving Isabel a stern glance.

"She didn't know," he said. "We met while we were in Vegas after Michael suggested I check out her showcase. With the Thanksgiving holiday approaching and because I had a meeting scheduled with Michael in New York next week, I thought I'd switch things up and come see the town they've told me so much about."

"You're a friend of Michael's?" Adaline asked.

"Miss Adaline is Michael's Mom," Isabel said softly.

Things finally clicked in the muck of her brain, and Isabel sucked in a breath. "And Everett is one of Michael's fraternity buddies."

And *this* was a prank. *That was it!*

They'd pranked Michael with the fake wedding pics from the *fake wedding chapel*, and now the two frat boys were pranking *her* by saying it was real.

A huff of a laugh escaped her as relief filled her body and she hid the sound with a cough, her mind scrambling to figure out how she could turn the tables back on them.

"A Columbia man," Cheryl said as though that alone sealed Everett's authenticity as a human being.

"I am," Everett said with a nod and a smile that brought sighs from all the Babes.

Izzy fought the urge to roll her eyes.

Men. Her handsome male cousins could do no wrong, and now all Everett had to do was smile and the Babes turned to mush.

Just like that he won them over. How was that possible?

She could do a handstand and balance a ball on her nose and still not get the smiling, approving looks from the Babes.

Then again, she supposed her balancing act wasn't exactly comparable to the overachieving men in her extended family. Did they all have to be doctors and architects and such?

That kinda put some pressure on a girl who'd dropped out of community college, beauty school, and real estate classes.

"Please, come sit down. Would you like something to drink? A snack?" Mary Elizabeth said. "As you can see, we have plenty left over. I'd be happy to make you a plate. The food was quite delicious."

"We definitely know how to throw a party," Rayna Jo added.

Isabel watched as Everett dipped his head and smiled until the dimples on his cheeks came out to play as a result. He shook his head after a glance down at her, however.

"Later, perhaps. Congratulations," he said to Amelia before his hand settled on Isabel's shoulder and gently squeezed.

"I'll let you get back to the party. Walk me outside," Everett suggested in a no-nonsense tone.

"Of course." Izzy glanced at Amelia and found her bestie frowning much the way Allie was. Like she knew this wasn't a normal visit from a normal friend and that things just weren't...*normal.*

But they didn't know what she knew, and when she got her hands on Michael for undoubtedly setting up this little scheme...

"Ladies, enjoy the rest of your evening," Everett said. "I'm sorry to have intruded."

"Nonsense. You haven't bothered us at all, and I'm sure you were excited to see Izzy. I hope we'll see you again soon?" her mama asked. "I know, come back tomorrow. We have all this food. I'll have a brunch for everyone. Michael and his brother included," she said. "You must come."

A chorus of pleases erupted from the Babes, and after another glance down at her, Everett nodded.

"Of course. I'd be honored."

"Ten-ish?" her mother suggested.

"Yes, ma'am. I'll be here."

Everett kept his hand on Izzy's shoulder, and now that he'd agreed to return and was free to go, he turned them both toward the front door. The moment they stepped out of sight and earshot, she grabbed his hand and shoved it off of her with a glare. "You should be ashamed of yourself."

"For meeting your family?"

"For this prank! *That* wasn't funny. You almost had me," she growled as she yanked the front door open and walked out.

"I don't understand. What do you mean?"

"When you said—" She stopped and waited until he'd closed the door behind them. "Look, you're team Izzy, you hear me?"

"Isabel—"

"It's just Izzy. Now, how are we going to turn this around on Michael again?"

"Ah," he said softly. "Isabel, it's no prank."

Everett made the statement and crossed his arms over his broad chest as he stared down at her. Izzy had never felt short at five six, but with him towering a solid ten inches above her, she felt small and feminine and more than a little angry that she couldn't take her frustration out on him by kicking him in the shins like she wanted. "Ha ha. *Enough.* We are not married. Michael put you up to this after we pranked him with those pics, so let's hurry up and think of a way we can turn this around. I'm not going down without a fight."

Everett looked around the porch before taking a step closer.

"Isabel, I am not pranking you. We are legally married."

Silence settled between them where they stood on the far side of the porch. A car rolled slowly down the driveway, the woman behind the wheel one of Amelia's work friends.

Izzy managed a smile and a small wave despite the fist once more squeezing her chest. "That's not funny," she said through her gritted teeth.

"I'm not trying to be."

A second passed. Then several more. The look on his face... "*What?*"

Izzy watched as Everett placed one hand on his hip and lifted the other to rub over his face and through his hair. He seemed to consider his words carefully, which made her even more nervous. Either he was a very good actor or Everett meant what he said.

Please, God, let him be an actor.

"Apparently we entered the wrong chapel."

No, no, no... She shook her head repeatedly, unable to accept his words. "No," she said, uncomfortable with the sudden turn this morning after talk had taken. "Look, Everett, I don't know what this is, but enough already. Joke's over."

He leaned a broad shoulder against the side of the house and crossed his arms over his chest. And heaven help her, but her eyes nearly bugged out of her head at the sight of his muscles straining the confines of his shirt. He might be a businessman but he stayed in shape.

"Isabel..."

Everett's voice lowered to a level she recognized. It was one her father had sometimes used with her growing up when he wanted her to focus on his words and really listen because whatever he said was important.

"No. No, you're... Look, it was fun but we both know exactly what that night was. I-I mean, you're in New York and I'm here and...I don't *do* that kind of thing so if you think I do and that you can come here for another round... I was just... It *won't* happen again, okay? Not that you've said you want to, but I'm saying it won't so...there."

She watched as his frown deepened before he

pulled a folded stack of papers from his rear pocket and held them out to her.

She eyed them like a snake but reluctantly accepted them, giving him another glare while unfolding the pages, recognizing them instantly. "Okay, so? Fake wedding, fake marriage certificate. We also had fake flowers and a fake dress and tux. It was part of the package from the *fake* chapel that took the *fake* pictures we sent Michael."

"Except that it wasn't fake," he murmured. "I'm just as surprised as you, Isabel. However, it doesn't change the truth. After I returned to New York, my assistant found the paperwork in my briefcase and immediately researched the chapel. The one we'd intended to go to was located next door to this one," he said, tapping the top of the papers she held. "We entered the wrong one."

"No."

"Yes."

"*Nooo,*" she said, horror sinking into her bones like a ship into the Atlantic. "You can't be... You're *serious?*"

"Would you like to call them to confirm?" he asked, digging into another pocket to retrieve his cell phone and holding it out to her.

She squeezed her eyes shut and pressed a hand to her chest to rub hard, the papers crumpled in her fist.

Inhale one.

Exhale two.

Now was totally the time to panic. "How could we not notice? We got there a-and you opened the door."

Married. She was *married?*

"I know I did. All I can say is that I was totally distracted by you," Everett said.

"You're blaming me?"

"*No.* No, I meant—"

"Forget it. It apparently happened, which means we screwed up, but that's what we'll tell a judge. We'd had a few drinks, it was supposed to be a joke and we...we can get it annulled."

"You can't get an annulment when the marriage has been consummated."

Fire rushed through her body and up into her face, and even though she'd turned thirty-two on her last birthday and was hardly a schoolgirl, the fact they'd most *definitely* consummated things left her blushing. "D-divorce then," she added in a small voice while avoiding his gaze.

It would be impossible to keep such a thing from her family but maybe, somehow, she could?

Everett inhaled and looked decidedly uncomfortable. So much so a knot formed in the pit of her stomach. "What? *Whaaaat?*" she asked when he didn't immediately respond.

He glanced over his shoulder into the window where the Babes' and Amelia's muffled voices could be heard through the glass panes. She'd closed the door for privacy, but given the number of women lingering post-party and the spiked punch that had been consumed, the party continued through cleanup if the giggling and laughter heard outside of the house was any indication.

"We have to talk about that."

"What's to talk about? Everett, this was a prank on my cousin that backfired big-time. We didn't intend for it to be real, so of course we're getting divorced."

"I hear what you're saying."

The way he said the words made her think of some sort of conflict negotiation crap no doubt learned in a boardroom somewhere. But there was nothing to negotiate here. It wasn't like they could stay married!

"And what you're saying is true, but I think we should wait before we rush into a divorce as quickly as we rushed into the marriage."

She blinked. Then blinked again while absorbing his words. "We didn't rush into anything. We didn't mean to actually... I knew you what? Four or five hours before we went to that chapel because I won the bet? Everett, this isn't a reality show. We have to take care of this."

"You're right. It isn't. But we're waiting."

"Oh, I beg to differ," she said with a rush of exasperation.

"Isabel, please. Hear me out. We need to slow down and consider all the possibilities and the ramifications before we move forward with anything."

Possibilities and ramifications? "Like what? What could make this worse?"

"What if you're pregnant?"

Gobsmacked, she nearly stumbled even though she stood still. "Pregnant?"

She'd been so focused on forgetting about him and Vegas that...

"We were both very much caught up in the moment, and while I've never done such a thing, conception is a possibility."

The air left her lungs in a rush, and even though she'd realized after the fact that there *might* a chance, slim though it was given the timing, hearing it spelled out in no uncertain terms just, well, sucked. And made her question her thinking.

She'd come home so exhausted by the trip and all the ideas for her new projects, getting ready for the baby shower and *avoiding* thoughts of Everett and Vegas, that by the time she considered a trip to the pharmacy, she'd then reconsidered.

Because even though Plan B was meant to prevent conception, a part of her brain couldn't get over the fact that *if* it had already happened in the short time span... She couldn't do that. Not after watching Amelia and Lincoln try so hard to conceive the baby she carried.

She was thirty-two, after all. And maybe she didn't make a normal living like everyone else, but she did okay, and what if this was her chance for a baby with someone strong and handsome, intelligent? A good guy? Regardless of whether or not he decided to take part in the baby's life.

But that wasn't something she could admit to a stranger. "Fine. So...I suppose we can wait until we know. I'll take a pregnancy test as soon as...soon," she muttered.

And because she really *wasn't* the type to do the whole tipsy one-night stand thing, she forced herself to voice the words that left her face flaming and her body pulled taut. "Do I need to...worry about anything else?"

Everett stretched out a hand and gently cradled her hot cheek in his palm, his thumb stroking over her cheekbone in a way that left a shivery ache behind.

Yeah, *that's* why they'd wound up in her hotel room. Because when that thumb stroked down her cheek and under her chin to gently tip her face toward his, her knees nearly buckled despite the horror of their conversation.

"No. No worries."

"Good," she said, exhaling the breath she didn't realize she'd held. "N-neither d-do you." Maybe it was a sign of the times, but that didn't make their conversation any easier. But after her last boyfriend had cheated on her, she'd wanted to make sure he hadn't done more damage.

"I don't know what you're thinking, but Vegas was a novelty for me as well, Isabel. I've never... forgotten myself that way."

Awkward silence descended between them, and she took a step back to get some breathing room as she tucked her hands into the pockets of the loose dress she wore.

Everett had to be lying. He couldn't look like that and not have women throwing themselves at him.

Doesn't mean he takes them up on it.

But what kind of man didn't?

Oh, she so wasn't going to go there. "So, um, I guess we wait and... I'll let you know when I find out. I'm sorry I didn't respond when you called a-and texted. I thought... I'm not sure what I thought, but it's been a crazy week. I'm sorry you had to make a trip here just because I was stubborn. You could've left a voicemail, though."

"I believe this news is best delivered in person."

Yeah, she could see that. Izzy stared up at him and wondered at the expression she saw in his gaze. Like he wanted to say something but it wasn't the right time. But good grief, what more could be said?

She didn't dare let herself wonder what else could go wrong.

"I didn't mind the trip. In fact, I plan to stay in town while we sort this," he said, his dark brown gaze holding hers in a stare that made butterflies flutter low in her belly. "Perhaps you would show me around while I'm here?"

She glanced toward the door and the house beyond. "Um. Everett, I don't think that's a good idea."

"Afraid you won't be able to keep your hands off your husband?"

Despite the chill in the evening air, sweat trickled down her back beneath the dress she wore, her entire body flushing from the images of Vegas that popped into her head at his words. There was that truth. Because even though he'd dropped a bomb on her by showing up in Carolina Cove, she'd be lying if she said she couldn't imagine snuggling up against his broad chest so he could keep her from thinking about the consequences that had brought him here in the first place.

He wasn't the only one totally distracted.

"I think it's a great idea," he said with an enticing smile.

Yeah. Turned out the Babes weren't the only ones impacted by those dimples. "I'm afraid I'm too busy. I-I have to work, t-to catch up on projects. It's my livelihood," she added defensively. "I don't create, I don't eat."

"Mmm. You wouldn't be trying to avoid me, would you, Isabel?"

"Why would I do that?" She flicked her tongue

over her too dry lips and barely suppressed a groan when she watched his gaze lower.

His rumbling chuckle made her toes curl.

"I'll see you tomorrow then."

"Wait, I just said I can't. Everett—"

"For the brunch."

She blinked at the reminder and then wanted to pull her hair out at the thought of spending quality time inside the house with the Babes and her family assessing and critiquing them as a couple. "Right. You can't just come up with an excuse to get out of it?"

"Why would I? Your family and friends are charming. I'd like to get to know them better."

"*Why?*" That's the last thing she wanted. "Everett, you'll give them the wrong impression. They'll think we're... They'll think we're *dating*."

"Okay."

Okay? "It's not okay. Look, this marriage thing is going to be our secret, right? I mean, we're not going to go telling people we screwed up on such an epic level," she lowered her voice to a raw whisper, "and actually got married by accident. Right?"

"That would bother you?"

"Considering my family already thinks I'm a failure in the most general terms, yeah, it would." She ran a hand through her hair to get it off her hot neck. "I don't need to give them more proof that I have done some really stupid things. I'd never live it down."

He seemed to ponder her words and finally nodded.

"I'll keep our secret...for now."

A rush of air left her chest and she nodded. She'd figure out a way to keep him quiet later if it came to that, but at least he wouldn't spill their embarrassing tale for the moment. "Good. Okay, so now we have to make sure Michael hasn't told anyone. I don't think he has or my mother and the Babes would've said something to me already," she said. "So all we have to do is tell Michael to keep the prank to himself, and if he has already told anyone, we can go along with the prank story while we wait for the test results and work on getting a *discreet* divorce."

"If you're not pregnant."

She blinked at him, at the tone he'd used. "Either way."

One thick dark eyebrow lifted at her words.

"I don't agree to that."

"What? Everett, pregnant or not, we can't stay married. I don't even know you."

Muffled laughter filtered through the closed windows and door once more, and she turned a wary eye that way.

"One step at a time, Isabel."

She liked the sound of her name on his lips. The

way his deep voice— *Stop it.* "Nu-uh. Our first step is a pregnancy test and a *divorce.*"

"People have married with less in common than we have."

She stared up at him with wide eyes. He couldn't mean that.

"Is this about control? I wouldn't keep a child from their father."

His gaze suddenly narrowed, and she watched as Everett abruptly stretched out a hand and gently grasped her nape, lowered his head, and pressed his lips over hers, silencing her before she had a chance to utter a complaint or—

"Ahem," Tessa said from the yard behind them. "Don't mind me. Just heading home. Good night, y'all. Don't do anything I wouldn't do."

Everett released her and Isabel pulled away, gasping at the sudden kiss yet thankful that Everett had undoubtedly heard Tessa and taken matters into his own hands—lips—to keep her from saying something they'd then have to explain.

Out of all the Babes, Tessa was considered the wildest, only because she'd been married three times and had babies by each man.

But in that moment?

Izzy couldn't help but wonder if Tessa's words weren't a warning of things to come. Or a statement of the past?

Once Tessa had walked down the driveway and

over to the boardwalk out of hearing range, Izzy exhaled. "Everett, be reasonable. You can't be serious about staying married regardless of whether or not I'm pregnant, are you?"

"Mmm. I should go as well." He dipped his head in a nod and murmured a good night.

She watched him go, gaping after him and following him to the edge of the porch steps. "That's it? You're leaving? Everett? *Are you?*"

CHAPTER FOUR

E verett pretended not to hear Isabel's quietly hissed questions about remaining married and left her to the baby shower details. He was quite sure she'd have a slew of questions fired her way once she reentered the house, but given her determination to pretend what had happened hadn't, he left her to navigate the questions however she saw fit.

Instead of returning to the house where Jacob and Tomas waited, he took the boardwalk to the first bridge over the dunes, his thoughts souring his mood as he tried to sort through the risks versus the rewards of his plans.

His gut told him he had an uphill battle where Isabel was concerned, but that challenge drew him. She wasn't a pretentious socialite trying to entrap him. Quite the opposite, in fact.

After all, he had been the one to reach out and open the chapel door for her. If anyone was to blame for the mistake, she could argue he had done this to her.

Everett frowned down at the sand gathered at the end of the bridge. He wasn't exactly dressed for a walk on the beach, but at the bottom of the bridge was an unoccupied bench he made his own.

He needed more time to think. To come up with the arguments that would need to be made to battle his way through the next few weeks, if not months.

Isabel's surprise that he might want anything other than a divorce shouldn't have felt like a slight but it had. Apparently he was okay to sleep with but not marry? It was quite the turn of tables for him and what he'd experienced since growing into the man he'd become.

He realized she based her statements on their lack of familiarity, but from the moment they'd met at the gallery in Las Vegas, they shared an ease. Not to mention more than a healthy dose of chemistry he found highly unique. Something he felt they could definitely work with and build on. It was one thing to find himself accidentally married to someone but quite another for it to be someone he found stunningly attractive.

Her smile, her scent. The way she'd twist her hair around a finger when she talked. How she lit up when she laughed.

But what were the odds she truly didn't know who he was when Google was only a few taps away? The thought brought a fresh wave of awareness that made him sit forward on the bench as it rushed over him.

Was it possible?

Isabel hadn't seemed to recognize his name in Vegas, other than to acknowledge that they both knew Michael. The thought of her not knowing his identity as a businessman or his financial status appealed on a level that made him want to go back to the house and kiss her senseless so that, if she hadn't already googled him, she wouldn't, so she'd never look at him the way women tended to do. He was more than a bank account and society pages. More than his wealth and business acumen.

Her lack of awareness, if true, was a clean slate, one he could use to get to know her and she him before the stresses of his financial status became a thing. Divorce, the news that he'd mistaken a real wedding chapel for a fake one wouldn't go unobserved by his peers and colleagues. If word got out, he risked not only his professional reputation but the trust his associates placed in him. More than money was at stake and tipped the scales toward staying married even more.

But he had another reason as well, one that went way deeper than mere image. Isabel's questions were valid. Could two strangers make it work? Would it be worth the battle? Or a failure in the end, regardless? Could he persuade her to take a chance?

For someone whose inner dialogue insisted failure wasn't an option, he didn't like the odds.

Seagulls squawked overhead as they found their homes and the night quieted around him. Waves crashed against the shore, and the last remaining shards of color disappeared from the sky to leave a quiet haze of blue-gray darkness that acted as an odd veil of comfort.

Once again he found himself enjoying the peace of anonymity. A few people still lingered on the beach, though not nearly as much as before, and no one paid him any attention.

Couples walked hand in hand in the surf. Young families with flashlights released delighted squeals when they discovered crabs emerging from the sand. He was no one here. Just another person enjoying the beach, and it was the best feeling he'd had for a while.

Since Vegas.

Yet another gift Isabel had given him, whether she knew it or not.

Everett remained on the bench and watched the goings-on, something in his heart tugging at the sights and sounds, at the emptiness he'd felt in his life for so long. A hole that couldn't be replaced with work or exercise.

Isabel fascinated him. The moment he'd met her,

she'd drawn him in with her bright smile and gray eyes. The unusual color made him think of a stormy sky, of lightning and wind and unknown adventure, her energy blasting through the air around her. Whenever she talked about her art and her plans for future work, she glowed from within, drawing him in until he hadn't been able to look away.

Isabel's sultry laugh and a mere glance from beneath her long, *natural* lashes had brought him to his knees. And when they'd gotten back to her room...

In his thirty-eight years, he'd never experienced anything as heady or as intoxicating. Which meant if he planned to see this through...

He pulled out his phone and found Michael's information in his contacts. Two rings later, his friend and colleague's voice filled the air.

"Hey, Everett, what's up?" Michael asked.

"Does Isabel know who I am?" Everett asked, getting straight to the point.

"Uh...she knows we've worked together, but I'm not sure how many details she knows."

"Does she know I'm a billionaire?"

"I haven't said anything specific since I don't talk about work except in general terms, but anyone or the internet could tell her that."

"Yeah, I know. But is that something she'd do? Look me up?"

Silence followed the question and Everett bit

back his frustration. Some things weren't meant to be public. It was no one's business how much money he had or who he'd dated in the past. His private life was private, and he wished he could keep it that way.

"Not necessarily. Izzy doesn't focus on those types of things. That doesn't mean one of her sisters or friends won't check you out though. What's going on?"

He thought about his conversation with Isabel about keeping their secret and hesitated, unsure of how much to reveal.

"Look, Everett, it's pretty obvious you're into her. You wouldn't be here if you weren't. What's going on?"

Everett inhaled and decided to take a chance, despite the risk it could pose. Michael was Isabel's cousin. If he talked, she would be hurt. "It turns out the chapel wasn't fake."

A huff of a laugh escaped Michael, but when Everett didn't comment further, he heard Michael inhale sharply.

"Come on. You can't be serious."

Everett ran a hand over his face and rubbed his eyes. "Have you told anyone about those pictures? The prank?" Isabel didn't want her family to know, but the truth would come out eventually. Such things always did.

"No. I've been working on a deadline and had my

head buried all week, so I haven't been around anyone. Nose to the grindstone and all of that. You're really married?"

"Yes. I didn't notice it wasn't the right entrance." Because truth be told, she'd been the distraction he'd needed that night in more ways than one.

"So you've told Izzy? How's she taking it?"

"She avoided my calls all week but I told her this evening. She wants a divorce."

"And you don't?"

His silence said more than the word could've, and Everett waited for Michael's response.

"Wow. Okay, that took a turn I wasn't expecting. So what do you want from me?"

Everett pinched the bridge of his nose and pondered the question. "You know her. And I need to get to know her fast. What she likes, how to... romance her."

"Sounds more like a conversation to have with Marsali Jones, not me."

The name rang a bell and suddenly pieces clicked in his brain. Marsali Jones. Recently married to Hollywood superstar Oliver Beck. The man had given up Hollywood for her and moved to Wilmington to start his own production company. It had been all over the news and tabloids alike. No wonder the woman had looked familiar. That and the fact she was front and center on bookshelves for her bestselling novel on dating. "She was at the baby shower for Isabel's friend."

"Yeah, probably so," Michael said. "I believe Izzy met Marsali when she hired Marsali to matchmake Amelia."

Interesting. It definitely sounded like a story he wanted to hear more of, especially if he could get some dating pointers—for his wife. "Any other suggestions?"

"Everett... are you sure you want to do this?"

"My intentions are honorable, Michael. Now that it's happened, I'd like to make the best of it."

"Are you sure you don't just want to save face? It was an honest mistake. Your pride might have to take a hit. That's just life."

Everett stared out at the ocean. The water looked dark, the sky barely a lighter shade of gray. Everett knew he'd need his friend's support if things went the way he wanted them to. Isabel seemed close to her cousins, and given the sudden turn in their relationship, Everett knew he'd need the vetting Michael could provide.

Men in his position didn't *date*. His life didn't accommodate the normalcy of such a thing and hadn't for years. And if he wanted Isabel as anything more than an accidental wife, he'd have to use everything—everyone—at his disposal to make it happen. "She's different," Everett admitted finally. "Isabel has something I've not experienced before, and if we could build on that—without her knowing or caring about my financial status—that would be a plus."

"You like her."

"Yes. I do." Maybe it was crazy given the short time frame, but he was a man who'd built a billion-dollar empire by reading people. Understanding them in ways they sometimes didn't understand themselves. All it took was time and attention to detail, sources like Michael, to help the process along.

Silence filled the air once again before Michael released a loud exhale.

"Okay. If you mean that, I'll do what I can to help."

"Thanks."

"But don't hurt her," Michael continued. "We may not be officially related, but she's as close to a kid sister as I've got."

The warning came over the phone loud and clear. "Understood."

"That said, I can't think of a nicer guy. And you certainly couldn't get a better woman. She's one of the good ones, even if she is a little crazy."

He chuckled at the description. Maybe that's what drew him to her. Maybe he needed a little crazy and chaos in his life to keep him from becoming one of the old, stodgy, boring businessmen he saw staring back in the mirror on a daily basis.

"Where are you staying?" Michael asked.

Everett gave him the address and listened as his friend chuckled.

"Man, you do have it bad. That's only a few blocks away from her."

"It seemed prudent to be close by."

Another chuckle filtered over the phone before Michael said, "Ahhh, you are working fast. I just got a text for brunch tomorrow to meet Isabel's *new friend.*"

Everett smiled at the announcement, well able to imagine Isabel's frustration when he charmed her mother and the other Babes.

Yes, he'd heard the story of the Boardwalk Babes. And he couldn't wait to hear all the other stories they'd tell about his Isabel. He could already picture her sassy attitude and precocious self on the beach as a child.

"Guess I'll see you then."

Everett ended the call and left the bench to make his way back to the house. Tomas and Jacob paced the front deck as though watching for him, and he shook his head at their concern.

This wasn't New York. No one knew him here, and the odds of him getting kidnapped and ransomed were slim. Plus, it wasn't like he could accidentally get married again.

Everett made his way to the lower level of the house and then jogged up the steps inside rather than take the elevator. The two men met him in the combination kitchen/living area, and Everett could practically hear the grind of Jacob's teeth. "Miss me?"

"With all due respect, sir, what's gotten into you?"

Everett chuckled and opened the refrigerator door. "I think we're going to find out. What's to eat?"

CHAPTER FIVE

I zzy felt Amelia's gaze lock on her the moment she stepped back inside. Before anyone else could notice, however, Amelia waddled her pregnant self over as quickly as she could and grabbed Izzy's arm to lead her into her father's office. "Um, problem?"

"Who was that?" Amelia asked.

"He's just a friend."

Amelia crossed her arms over her bountiful chest and glared at her.

"Try again."

Izzy tried to maintain her cool but, given her newly married state, lost it. "You can't say a word."

"Izzy—"

"I mean it. Not. A. Word. Not to anyone. Not even your husband," Izzy said, knowing Amelia didn't like to keep things from Lincoln. In this case, she would have to make an exception.

"Fine."

"I mean it," Izzy said again.

"I get it. I promise."

Izzy held up her hand and Amelia rolled her eyes.

"Seriously?"

"Pinky swear...on your babies," she added for good measure.

Amelia gasped and slowly linked their fingers.

"You're scaring me. I won't say anything. Now what is going on and who was that?"

"He's... Everett is apparently my husband."

A bark of laughter burst out of Amelia before she caught sight of Izzy's expression and apparently realized she wasn't joking.

"*Husband?*"

"Shhhh!" Izzy moved toward the open office door and shut it behind them, flipping the lock for good measure before she nodded at Amelia. "It was a prank on Michael," she said, explaining how she'd met Everett in Vegas, their celebration, bet, and the whole shebang.

"But the chapel was legit," Amelia repeated, wide-eyed.

"Yup," Izzy said, drawing out the *P* with a pop.

"Oh my— *Izzy*. What are you going to do?"

Izzy shoved her hair off her face and once again

considered cutting it all off. One of these days... "He's been calling and texting, presumably to let me know but...I wouldn't respond. I mean, it was a one-time thing, which you know I never, ever do, and I was embarrassed by how I just up and left him in the shower."

"Thank God he could track you down though."

Izzy debated the thankful part, even though she got the gist of it. "I guess I didn't leave him a lot of choice. But Michael knows Everett and has worked with him. If Everett was a weirdo, I'm sure Michael wouldn't have told Everett to look me up at my show." She released the nail she hadn't realized she nibbled and grimaced. "Right?"

"Yes. That's totally true," Amelia mused. "Michael wouldn't tell someone untrustworthy to seek you out. So what happens now? Oh, of all times I can't skip work and come to that brunch. I'd love to be a fly on the wall."

"Me, too. I wish you could come for moral support if nothing else."

"Does that mean you're telling everyone tomorrow?"

"What? No. What gave you that idea?"

Amelia palmed her large belly and stroked like only an expectant mother would.

"You're not telling your family you're married?"

"Nope. Not if I can help it." Izzy shook her head several times for good measure. "Once we know for certain I'm not pregnant, we'll get a discreet divorce."

"Wow. Okay."

"What?"

"I mean, does that exist?" Amelia asked.

"Leave me some hope," Izzy said with a groan as she plopped into one of the side chairs along the office wall near the couch.

Amelia moved to join her, lowering herself to the couch with all the grace she could muster.

"I mean, the last thing I need is for my family to know I screwed up on that level of epic, you know?"

"It was an honest mistake."

"And the wedding night?" Izzy grimaced, face hot as she blinked at her friend and fought off her embarrassment. When she said she didn't do one-night stands, she meant it. And to have done one—literally one—and have it come back to bite her this way?

"Well, your parents might not approve, but there are worse things in the world. Let's get real here."

Izzy covered her face with her hands. "What have I done? This is my punishment."

"You're being silly. Punishment for what?" Amelia asked.

"For giving my parents such a hard time growing up. For dropping out of college and beauty school and all the other things I started and gave up on. This is the cherry on top, right here."

"Iz, you were trying to find your way. You always knew you wanted to be an artist, but from what you've told me, they pushed you into other things to deter you."

"They said I needed a way to pay the bills," Izzy said with a twist of her lips.

"Yeah, well, everyone has to find their own way. You've grown and matured and you're paying your own way now. That's the important thing."

"I guess. I mean, I've had some lean months, but thankfully I've learned the art of saving and want versus need."

"See? That's maturity."

"It also helps that London lets me work at the coffee shop if things are really bad, to help pay my rent."

"See? You're paving the way on your own, so don't sell yourself short. It'll all work out. Just wait and see."

"Yeah, well, until then, I have to get through tomorrow, and you know how the Babes will be at that brunch. Are you sure you can't ditch work?"

"Now who's wanting me to be irresponsible?" Amelia shook her head, a sorrowful expression crossing her face. "You're on your own. Sorry. Filming will be tricky tomorrow and there's no way I can miss it."

"Fine. Make me face the firing squad myself."

Amelia's chuckle filled the room and drew a reluctant smile from Izzy.

"Tell me more about Everett," Amelia ordered. "He's so—"

"Izzy! Where are you?" Sophia called, her voice echoing through the large house.

Izzy groaned but welcomed the interruption, whatever it took to steer clear of her *husband*. "In here! Sorry."

"You're not getting off that easily," Amelia said, lowering her voice as footsteps hurried down the hallway toward the office door.

"Duty calls," Izzy said, getting to her feet and rushing to open the door before Sophia could get there and realize it was locked. That would only bring more questions.

"Hey, Iz, have you seen— Oh, Amelia, your husband is here to drive you home. He mentioned you have an early day tomorrow."

"Yes, you do," Izzy said, desperate to take the attention off of herself and the topic of Everett.

"I'll help you out," Sophia said.

"You're not staying? Tomorrow is Saturday," Izzy said to her sister.

"Yeah, well, I'm not spending the night here for the same reason you don't want to have that brunch tomorrow," Sophia said sweetly, her smile as fake as they come.

"Ohhh? Does this mean you don't want to be grilled either? Who is he?" Amelia asked.

"Yeah, So-So," Izzy said, using the nickname for her middle sister she'd used since birth since neither she nor Allie had been able to pronounce Sophia's full name when they were toddlers and the nickname had stuck. "What don't *you* want Mom and the Babes to know?"

TESSA GLANCED up when a shadow blocked the light shining from the railing lining the boardwalk. A man stood nearby, a smile on his handsome face.

"Uh, hi. I'm sorry, I just... I had to come over here and say hello," he said in a deep voice. "May I join you?"

Tessa loved the safety of Carolina Cove and never worried about being on the boardwalk alone at night. She'd often walk down to the swings near the pier and swing for hours, watching the tourists and locals alike. She'd always found people watching to be addictive. "Do we know each other?" Tessa asked.

Thanksgiving was less than a week away, and even though she wouldn't spend the holidays completely alone thanks to her children, it would be yet another year where she'd wake up in the house alone. And even though it shouldn't bother her because she'd been here before, it did.

"May I?" The man waved his hand and indicated the empty space beside her.

"Uh, I suppose. Sure."

The man lowered himself beside her and seemingly noted the title of the book she'd pulled from her purse but hadn't bothered to open. Even with the reading light she also carried with her, she hadn't so much as flipped the cover, preferring to stare at the ocean and take in the sounds after the noise of so many at the shower.

"That's a good one," he said with a nod at her lap and the book atop it.

The book currently ranked number one on all the bestseller lists and should have held her attention like the man beside her suddenly did. But then, when given a choice between a book and person for company...

"My name is Kirk."

"Tessa," she said, wondering why someone at least ten years her junior would want to sit and talk to her.

"Do you like it?" he asked. "I found the main character a bit whiny."

Tessa laughed and realized he was right. "Me, too! I keep going though. The writer has a style that keeps me turning the page, so I'm overlooking that annoyance."

Kirk didn't seem to be in a rush to move along, and Tessa took a glance around, figuring the other benches and swings were full and he'd simply wanted a seat. Except, the one closest to her wasn't occupied at all. "Are you waiting for someone?"

"No."

"Oh."

Kirk ran a hand over his salt-and-pepper head and shot her a slow smile.

"Sorry. I shouldn't bother you, I suppose, but I'm trying hard to work up my nerve to ask you out. It's taking me longer than I thought it would."

A laugh bubbled out of her before she could stop it. "I think the lighting here has messed with your eyes, Kirk. You do realize I'm older than you, right?"

"Does that matter? You're beautiful. I noticed you sitting here as I walked down the pier and I...I don't know, I knew I had to meet you."

She tilted her head to one side and tried not to be flattered. "And now that you're close enough to realize I'm not a young woman, you're stuck trying to figure out a way to gracefully excuse yourself from the situation?"

"Have I tried to leave yet?"

His bright smile tilted his lips up at the corners and made his eyes twinkle from the lights around them. She couldn't tell what shade they were, only that they were dark. "Are you here on vacation?"

That was one of the problems with living in a beach town. Singles and family men alike came to visit, often looking for a little companionship or a vacation fling while they were in town but never anything more serious.

"I'm a local, actually."

"Really?" She wasn't sure why she was surprised but she was.

"Yeah. Well, okay, I'm a transplant originally, but I think five years makes me a local now. Does that mean you'll consider having dinner with me after all?"

Her heart raced in her sixty-two-year-old chest, and she couldn't help the surge of warmth his question brought. It was silly of her to think anything would come of it, but what would dinner hurt? An evening with a good meal and a handsome man for company?

"I can tell you want to ask, so I'll get it out of the way. I'm forty-nine."

Oh. Wow. *More* than ten years younger. "Kirk, I'm beyond flattered that you'd ask but I don't think—"

"Don't think," he said. "Just say yes. Come on, take a chance. You never know, I might be the man of your dreams."

"I don't even know you."

"Isn't that the point of dating? Getting to know someone?"

It was. And since her last husband had died several years ago, all she'd done was throw herself into work. After three strikes, she figured she was out of chances to find happily ever after.

Did she dare? Just for fun?

"Come on, beautiful. Say yes. We'll have dinner. Take a walk on the beach. Whatever you want," he said.

The engaging smile on his too handsome face and hopeful look she couldn't ignore left her nodding. "Okay, yes."

He clapped his hands together once in his excitement that she'd accepted his request, and she laughed at his exuberance.

She hoped she wasn't making an embarrassing mistake. "Tell me, Kirk. What do you do besides flatter old women on the boardwalk?"

Kirk reached across the expanse of the bench and plucked her hand from her lap, carrying it to his lips.

"I only see a beautiful woman. As for what I do..."

CHAPTER SIX

The following morning, Everett knocked softly on Izzy's door. He heard grumbling on the other side and smiled.

The door opened after a few thumps and Isabel's sleep-tousled head appeared. She wore a tank and shorts with a short, lightweight robe thrown on top. Seeing him on her doorstep, she hastily crossed the robe over her front and tied it.

"What are you doing here?"

"Escorting you to brunch," he said, entering her apartment without waiting on an invitation. When he stepped next to her, he held up a freshly brewed coffee from downstairs and watched as Isabel licked her lips before sinking her teeth into her lower one. The sight made him want to do that to her himself.

"You can't get on my good side with coffee."

"You sure about that?" he asked, tilting the cup to and fro to tease her.

She frowned harder, and he had a difficult time holding back a chuckle. Even grumpy, with her hair pulled up in a messy bun, she was beautiful.

"Gimme."

Another chuckle emerged from him, and he liked that she could pull that kind of response. He knew he took life far too seriously, but having grown up the way that he had, someone had needed to be serious. It was the only way of keeping his grandfather's legacy alive after his father's bumbling through women had nearly destroyed it in the early years.

Everett closed the door behind them and watched as she made her way over to a round, puffy chair. He studied her apartment with interest, wanting to take in every detail that might give him more insight into her.

The windows were covered in blinds but then had a gauzy fabric draped over them as well. Her faded blue velvet sofa held an assortment of pillows. Some furry, some sparkling, and some simply woven. The coffee table was made of driftwood covered with clear glass, and atop it was a stack of tabletop art books and what looked to be art supply catalogues.

The small living room backed up against the kitchenette, divided by a bar with a couple of stools. Her actual dining area was filled with an easel, table, crates, paints, canvas, tools, and other odds and ends piled high on every surface.

"Nosy much?"

The grumbled query brought his attention back to her, and he stared at the long stretch of her bare legs where she'd curled them up on the chair. "You love your art."

"My mother calls it a decorating nightmare."

"All I see is a need for more space."

"Yeah, well, space comes at a premium when you live at the beach." She took another sip of her coffee and eyed him over the rim. "Why are you here, Everett?"

He shoved his hands into the pockets of his casual slacks, an appropriate choice for brunch with her family at the beach, he thought, and tilted his head to the left as he regarded her. "I thought we should talk before heading over. Discuss our Vegas story in detail?"

She'd lifted the cup to her lips for another drink but froze at his words.

"I thought we'd agreed on keeping our stupid mistake a secret."

"We did. But at some point, someone could ask what we wound up doing in Vegas after your show."

Isabel squeezed her eyes shut and leaned her head back on the cushion behind her.

"Drinks. That's all we have to say," she said, running a hand over her hair. "And as far as staying married, we're *not*. Besides, what are the odds that my one and only one-night stand would result in a pregnancy?"

He could give her the statistics but doubted she actually wanted to hear them.

"As far as brunch goes, our story is that you know Michael, he mentioned me having a show there, and we met when you introduced yourself and had drinks after the show. *End* of story."

"Your aunt saw me kiss you last night."

"We're friends. No big deal."

"Do you kiss all of your male friends?" Jealousy spiked through him, a surprise to say the least. He'd never felt enough about a woman to be jealous of what she did or with whom, but here he sat with a woman he barely knew yet was married to, and the thought of her kissing other men made him want to growl and claim her like a caveman.

One slim eyebrow rose on her face, and he watched as she shrugged.

"I didn't kiss you. You kissed me. Don't do it again and we'll be fine."

He pondered her words for a moment but decided, in an effort to keep things honest, he had to say more. "Yeah, that doesn't work for me, Isabel."

He watched as she swallowed, the delicate muscles of her neck moving with the action.

"I'm sorry, what?"

He stood and moved over to where she sat,

stretching out a hand she reluctantly accepted, allowing him to pull her to her feet. "Go get ready. It's almost time for our date."

"We don't have a *date*. We have brunch—with my *mother*. Are you going to behave yourself?"

He grinned and lowered his head to brush a lingering kiss across her lips, reveling in the softness despite her sharp intake of breath. Point proven that he would steal kisses whenever he could, he released her and stepped back. "I guess not."

———

TESSA SMOOTHED a hand down the tunic dress she'd chosen to wear for the brunch, feeling every bit her age when her best friend's home began to fill with their children and grandchildren.

It wasn't that she was jealous of the girls, she'd been twenty and thirty something once herself. It was just that somewhere along the line she'd gotten *old*, and she'd never felt that as completely as she did this very moment.

What was she thinking, agreeing to go out with Kirk? Why on earth would she set herself up to be the subject of the island's gossip? Were women over sixty called cougars? Or something worse?

"Hey, you okay? What's that about?" Mary Elizabeth asked.

Tessa glanced at her friend and slowly crossed

the floor to accept the mimosa Mary Elizabeth held out for her. "What's what about?"

"That look."

"What look?"

"Uh-huh. What happened?"

Of all the Babes, Tessa was closest with Mary Elizabeth. Adaline and Rayna were twin sisters and always together, and while Cheryl was friendly with all five of the ladies, Tessa and Mary Elizabeth had always just been there for one another.

But knowing she needed to give her friend an answer that did *not* include Kirk, she said, "I saw him again."

Mary Elizabeth—MeMe—raised the delicately arched eyebrow Tessa had just waxed earlier that week and gave her a stare down as only a lifelong friend could. "And?"

"And...I was on a date and it made me uncomfortable. Why do I keep seeing *him*?"

"It's an island, Tessa. You're going to run into your ex-husband."

That had also occupied her mind on the walk here. What had *Bruce* thought of her date with Kirk? It was obvious to anyone with eyes that Kirk was younger.

Why do you care what he thinks?

Tessa rolled her head to one side to ease the tension. "I know but...during all these years, I haven't seen him that often. Now it's like he's everywhere I turn."

"I think the real question is why does it bother you?"

Tessa glared at her friend and shook her head. "Do not go there."

"It's a simple question."

"You're implying more."

"That's your conscience prodding you," Mary Elizabeth said, straightening from her leaning position against her gorgeous quartz countertop when Cheryl and her mother, Georgia, the last of the living Babe mothers, walked in. "Welcome! Ms. Georgia, I hope you came hungry."

"I did, my dear, I did," the ninety-two-year-old spitfire said. "I'm sorry I missed the shower for Isabel's sweet friend, but my volunteer group had snagged those tickets ages ago, and I couldn't back out on them."

Mary Elizabeth kissed Georgia's softly wrinkled cheek before stepping back so that Tessa could take her turn. All of the mothers—and fathers for that matter—had passed except for Ms. Georgia, and the loving woman had taken each of them as her own as only a loving mama could.

Much to Cheryl's chagrin, her mother wasn't always the polite southern belle she'd been raised to be. No, with age had come feistiness, and Ms.

Georgia was a woman who spoke her mind no matter the situation or the surroundings.

"It's fine. Amelia wouldn't have wanted you to cancel your plans," Mary Elizabeth said.

"Well, I left a gift for her in the foyer. Please give it to her and give her my best."

Tessa smiled at the woman's gesture and held up an empty glass. "Of course. Mimosa?"

"None for me," Cheryl said, going on to greet the others in the room. "Orange juice has been bothering me lately."

"I'll take one. Make it a double," Georgia said with a wink.

"Hadley sends her apologies as well," Cheryl said.

"You've talked to her?" Tessa asked, knowing Cheryl was concerned as to why her only child hadn't visited from Raleigh for nearly a year despite it only being a two-hour drive.

"Briefly. She says the kids are involved in absolutely everything, and she doesn't want to miss out since an empty nest looms," Cheryl said.

"Well, we can certainly understand that," Mary Elizabeth said. "Can't we, ladies? We've all been there."

"I would've held on to Zoey's legs as she left for college if I wasn't so afraid she'd kick her way free," Tessa offered as a joke. "Let Hadley enjoy what time she has left with her baby girl under her roof. I'm sure they'll be here once summer comes and things settle down after graduation."

"Exactly. One last hurrah and all of that," Mary Elizabeth said.

"So what were you two girls discussing when we walked in?" Georgia asked from the chair where she now sat. "You both looked awfully serious."

Mary Elizabeth shot Tessa a teasing look and ignored Tessa's head shake.

"Tessa keeps running into Bruce, and it's giving her the flutters."

"What's this now?" Cheryl asked, eyes going wide before narrowing shrewdly.

Tessa felt her face heat like a schoolgirl. "That wasn't nice," she said to MeMe. "And I'm not getting *any*thing," she said to the others. "I simply mentioned that in the last little while I keep running into him. Even though I've only run into him a handful of times over the years."

"Maybe it just means you've both stopped avoiding one another. It's about time," Rayna Jo said, joining the conversation as she moved to greet Georgia.

"Yes, well, the focus today is on Isabel, remember?" Tessa desperately tried to steer the conversation away from her first husband and back to something less personal. At least for her. "I just happened to spot Isabel *kissing* her friend yesterday evening as I left."

"Really?" Mary Elizabeth asked, a frown pinching her eyebrows together above her nose even though a sparkle entered her gaze.

"There's definitely something going on there," Tessa added. She felt a little guilty for throwing Izzy under the bus, so to speak, but desperate times and all of that.

"Let's hope we find out more today then," MeMe said. "He did make a good first impression, didn't he? Very mannerly, well dressed... Oh, a mother can only hope. Especially given the ones she's brought home before."

"The party's here," Michael called out as he and his fraternal twin, Logan, entered the house.

Greetings were returned from throughout the room, but Adaline separated herself from her husband's side and moved to greet her sons.

Handsome men, both of them.

As they made the rounds, the boys greeted Georgia and complimented her before helping themselves to drinks.

"So, we hear you know Everett," Mary Elizabeth said to Michael. "Tell us everything."

Michael had just taken a sip of his drink and smiled as he shook his head at them while lifting the glass and a single finger to point toward the door.

"I've got a better idea," he said after he'd swallowed. "Why don't you ask him yourself?"

ISABEL FELT every eye in the room lock on them the instant she and Everett walked into the kitchen area. She took a breath and pasted on a shaky smile, determined to get through the brunch and out of there as quickly as humanly possible.

Her nerves wouldn't last long, especially not after the kiss Everett had given her at her apartment before she'd hightailed it to her bedroom and locked the door behind her.

What was up with that?

How could Everett think they'd ever have anything more than Vegas? Not only were they strangers but he was a New Yorker, for pity's sake! And like any true southern girl, she hated the cold and snow.

The open windows carried the seventy-degree breeze that tousled the balloon arch remaining in the living room from last night's shower.

Had it only been last night?

With a start, she realized it had. Even though it felt like time traveled at warp speed.

And once today was over, Thanksgiving would be next.

With Everett determined to stay in town until she knew for sure she wasn't pregnant, which factored into the holiday with gut-clenching accuracy.

"Everyone, this is Everett Drake, Isabel and Michael's friend," Mary Elizabeth stated, introducing him.

"I'm Izzy's father, Adam," Adam said. "Welcome. Come meet everyone, Everett."

Isabel watched as Everett left her side to join her father and the other men, but not until after a gentle squeeze of her arm. That came after he slid his hand from her lower back, neither of which went unnoticed by any of the women in the room.

Izzy stifled a groan and fought the urge to turn on her heel to leave but forced herself to approach the group of women eyeing her like they mentally sized her for wedding dresses and booked venues.

The Babes surrounded the chair where Ms. Georgia sat, Isabel's sisters nearby, looking as curious as the mothers.

She hadn't had any luck getting an answer out of Sophia last night as to what *she* was keeping from the Babes. Hopefully she'd be able to corner her sister sometime soon and try again. Like Izzy, Sophia knew to keep her private life private or else suffer the consequences of the Babes getting involved on an even larger scale than if they found something out on their own.

Rayna Jo's daughters, Dara and Devon, rarely came to events seeing as how Devon lived in New York City working as a television show host and Dara lived—where was it now?—and worked for a private security company called Guardian Group. Only Izzy, Allie, and Sophia were local, as well as Michael and Logan.

That meant when it came to family functions of any sort, they carried the slack of the others, as their attendance was *mandatory* rather than optional.

Which brought them to today.

Izzy greeted Ms. Georgia and asked about her health before turning to face the sea of women waiting for her to give them the details of her companion. Isabel rolled her eyes and sighed. "Really? I don't even get a drink first?"

Sophia grinned silently and quickly handed Izzy a filled flute.

"He's very handsome."

"Those dimples!"

"His eyes are quite compelling, too. It's those dark, sooty lashes," Tessa added. "They give him a bit of mysterious air, don't you think?"

"The hot body doesn't hurt," Ms. Georgia stated in a stage whisper that could've been heard on the West Coast.

Surprised laughter burst out of the Babes—minus Cheryl—as well as several of the men across the room blatantly eavesdropping on them, and Isabel shook her head and grimaced. What on earth would Everett think of them after this?

Her father lifted his glass toward her with

another low chuckle and then went on to introduce Logan and Michael's father to Everett.

Izzy tried. She really did. She tried hard not to look at Everett, but after a moment's stubbornness, her gaze shifted with a mind of its own and found his locked on her instead of the men surrounding him.

Direct. Amused.

Sensual?

He'd heard every word.

"Good golly, the last time a man looked at me like that, I married him," Tessa said, lifting a hand to fan her face dramatically.

Izzy had lifted her glass and taken a hasty drink only to choke on the citrus and champagne once Tessa's statement registered. She coughed and her eyes watered, her blurred vision catching sight of Everett's wide smile. More proof her father wasn't the only one eavesdropping.

"Girls, you're embarrassing poor Izzy," Ms. Georgia said, her gaze sharp as a tack.

"It's fine. Wrong pipe," she managed, voice husky from coughing.

"Good. Because I'd like to meet your young man," Ms. Georgia said.

"He's not mine, Ms. Georgia. He's just a friend." She'd just uttered the words when Everett's hand slid possessively around her waist and settled on her hip.

"Are you all right?"

Izzy heard the Babes and Ms. Georgia sigh with approval at his inquiry. "Fine."

Izzy stepped away from Everett only to find him moving with her, their hips and thighs brushing in the process. Her face heated up even more when a tingle of awareness zapped through her body.

"You must be Ms. Georgia," Everett said in his deep, rumbling voice. "It's a pleasure, ma'am."

Everett released Izzy's waist long enough to take the hand Ms. Georgia held out to him and squeeze it gently.

"You are a handsome devil, aren't you?" Ms. Georgia said.

Everett chuckled and Izzy rolled her eyes at the way the group of women practically swooned at his feet. Enough already. "Mama, is the food ready? I have work to do today."

"Isabel, don't be rude. We're just getting to know your guest," her mother said.

Izzy fisted her hands and managed another smile. If she wasn't so afraid of what Everett might say while she wasn't around, she'd leave him there and get out while the Babes were occupied and the gettin' was good. "Maybe our guest is hungry, Mama," she suggested sweetly, trying her best to get things moving. It was rude to talk with a mouthful after all.

"I know I am," Michael said as he joined them. "Hey, squirt."

She glared up at her cousin. "Really? Will I ever

outgrow that nickname?" she asked, irritable but uncaring. Her last nerve frayed to a single thread, and she had a feeling tying it in a knot and hanging on for dear life wouldn't work. Not today. Not with Everett looking at her like he wanted to...

"Never." Michael lowered his head and kissed her cheek, looking down at her with amusement.

"Fine, let's eat then, shall we?" her mother said. "I have things set up buffet style in the dining room. Right this way."

The group moved as a whole to file into the other room, and Michael offered Ms. Georgia his arm to escort her.

Everett turned to stare down at Izzy, the last to move toward the doorway.

"Kissing cousins?" he asked her.

A laugh bubbled out of her before she could stop it. "Seriously? Ew. Not everything you read about the south is true, you know."

He chuckled. "Just checking."

"Would it bother you if we had? It's not like Michael and I are actually cousins"—she lowered her voice—"nor are you and I a couple."

One of Everett's thick eyebrows shot high, but he didn't argue her statement even though it looked like he wanted to.

In fact, his lack of comment had the feel of something more. Like he knew something she didn't but wasn't going to let her in on the secret.

What the heck?

"Shall we?"

"Everett, stop. What are you doing?"

"Escorting you to brunch."

"Yeah, but why are you looking at me like that? Why are you behaving like we're more than just friends?"

The smile that stole over his lips brought to mind that night in Vegas, and she rolled her eyes, ignoring his arm and huffing out a breath as she started to stomp away.

Everett snagged her elbow in a gentle grip, spinning her around and wrapping his other hand at the nape of her neck, using both to pull her to him. He closed his lips over hers, silencing her gasp with an all-too-tempting kiss that left her head whirling even though it lasted mere seconds.

Against her lips, he murmured, "We aren't 'just friends,' Isabel. The sooner you realize that, the better."

Face hot, she struggled to fill her lungs with air as she stumbled her way into the dining room on his arm, wondering if everyone could tell they'd just kissed while their backs were turned.

She'd never been a PDA kinda girl but that?

How was it possible that a single kiss, lasting only seconds, could *rock* her? That wasn't normal, was it?

She'd kissed her share of boys and men over the

years, and not once did she ever remember those kisses being as drugging or intoxicating as Everett's. An instant *zing* that shot through her like lightning.

While some might think that was a good thing, she wasn't so sure that was the case.

"Aren't you hungry, sweetheart?" her mother asked.

"Mom, she's date eating, hello," Allie said in a teasing voice.

Isabel glanced up and shot her sister a glare. Now wasn't the time for sibling rivalry. She needed support, not more attention brought to them. "I had coffee."

"Coffee isn't breakfast," her mother said, *tsking*.

Everett silently handed her a plate he'd filled with fruit and a tiny, flaky croissant along with a mini quiche.

"Eat."

This time he got her glare—and she got a dimpled smile that left her knees weak and pulse pounding. What was it about domineering men that got to her?

CHAPTER SEVEN

Everett couldn't stop the smile forming on his face as he and Isabel left the Shipleys' and silently walked away from the house.

"Would you like to come see where I'm staying?" he asked. "It has a great view."

Isabel didn't answer but her pace picked up, forcing him to adjust his stride to match.

"I think things went well back there, don't you?"

"Ha!"

He didn't bother restraining his chuckle and continued to match pace with her ever-increasing stride. "I'd say I fit in quite well. Your family's adjustment to me being your husband shouldn't be too much of a stretch."

She stopped so fast he nearly stumbled in his effort to do so as well. Turning to face her, he took note of her fisted hands and the way her chest rose and fell with every exasperated breath.

Before leaving her apartment, she'd changed into a flowy maxi dress with a V neck and pockets, along with low-heeled boots. She wore a long necklace and dangly earrings, and he liked the simple yet elegant look on her.

"They aren't going to know you're...that we're... They *can't*."

"Because?"

She blinked up at him at the question.

"We can't have this conversation on repeat. Everett, what's the endgame here?"

"Pardon?"

"The endgame," she repeated. "What do you want? Why do you continuously say these things when you know our marriage was an accident that *will* be corrected as soon as I can hire an attorney since you seem determined not to?"

He shoved his hands into his pockets and regarded her from behind his sunglasses. "Isabel, I believe we can make our marriage work."

"*What?*"

Sensing a couple coming up behind them, he gently snagged her elbow in his hand and tugged her over to an empty bench. "You said you didn't want your parents to know you'd messed up."

"So?"

"You're not the only one who doesn't like failure, Isabel," he said. "And even though we didn't intend to get legally married, now that we are, I see no reason why we can't move forward as a couple and see where things go, regardless of whether or not you're pregnant."

"You're joking."

"I'm not." He tugged at his ear before yanking the sunglasses off in the hope that she could see his sincerity. "Are you seeing someone?"

The report hadn't mentioned a boyfriend, but given that it had been culled so hastily, there was always a margin for error.

"No, but—"

"Neither am I. So what's the issue? You're free. I'm free. We know we're compatible sexually—"

"We. Are. S*trangers*."

He nodded as she emphasized every word. "That can be easily rectified."

"You think it's that easy to make a marriage work?"

"I think it's a start. Let's spend as much time together as we can, get to know one another, and see what happens."

"Everett, I have a life. I have to get back to work. My rent—"

"I'll pay your rent."

"For the love of—"

She closed her eyes and mouth in obvious frustration and told him what he could do with his offer to cover her rent without saying a word.

"What do you want, Isabel? You didn't find me abhorrent in Vegas, so what's stopping you from exploring this opportunity now?"

Everett watched as she bit her lip again and worried it between her teeth until the flesh turned white. He forced his gaze off the succulent treat and back to her beautiful gray eyes.

"You're not abhorrent. But all of this is just... We'd be crazy to think for even a moment that a *prank* could turn into something more."

"What if our mistake wasn't a mistake but fate stepping in?"

She opened her mouth to reply but then closed it without speaking. He wished he could delve into her thoughts. Read her mind and get insight into what-ever it was holding her back. Isabel didn't strike him as a woman reined in by her fears.

"You aren't the type of man who believes in fate," she said finally.

He wasn't. But there was something different and unique about this situation that he couldn't put a finger on. There was more at work here than happenstance.

"Everett, what would people think?"

"The woman I met in Las Vegas wasn't afraid of what people might think."

She shot him a side look from beneath her lashes.

SEASCAPES AND VEGAS MISTAKES   111

"She was drunk."

"No, she wasn't. Neither of us were and you know it."

Her eyes widened. "You're saying subconsciously we *knew* that was a fake chapel and did it anyway?"

He chuckled at her horror and shook his head. "I wouldn't go as far as that. I'm simply saying...I've come to realize certain things happen in life whether we're prepared for them or not. Call it what you like, but what if our walking into the wrong chapel is part of our story?"

"What do you mean?"

"Well, if it hadn't happened, we would've gone our separate ways, slipped back into our lives, and I wouldn't be here now. But it did. And I am," he stated firmly, dipping his head to force her to hold his gaze when she started to look away. "And that crazy story of how we accidentally got married can be the thing we tell people later because it worked out."

"We don't know that it would."

"We don't know that it won't. We get to decide how to proceed with the chance we've been given. And the effort we put into making it work."

A spark of hope bloomed inside of him when she seemed to give his statement intense thought. "Isabel—"

"It's just Izzy," she said with a small shake of her head. "Everyone calls me Izzy."

"Isabel," he said softly again, stroking a hand over

her cheek and using his touch to gently lift her face toward his. "I'm not asking for blind devotion. We can take it slow. Just...spend time with me."

"You mean while you're here, u-until we know whether or not I'm pregnant?"

She appeared to think that was a more reasonable request, and since he'd pushed her enough for the day, he knew to take it for a win. "That's a start," he said, refusing to commit to anything short-term when long term was his goal.

"I suppose...I suppose it wouldn't hurt, but my family will get the wrong idea. Then when you leave, I'll be the one dealing with all of the questions after you're gone."

He pondered that for a moment and understood her concern. Though in his case, he couldn't imagine anyone caring enough to question him about his feelings for her. Yet another difference in her family and his. "We'll be as discreet as we can for now."

She shook her head and shot him a frown.

"What?" he asked.

"You make me want to say yes but the island is a fishbowl. Privacy doesn't exist. Everyone knows my parents and the Babes. No matter where we go, someone will probably recognize me and then call the Babes to get the scoop and—"

"We'll deal with that when it happens."

Her shoulders slumped and he had a feeling he was wearing her down.

"Everett...you know you're handsome. You dress nice, which means you obviously have some cash to spend. You're smart and...you could walk into any bar or restaurant in town and get any woman you want. Why not just get a divorce and be done with it? Why me?"

Why her, indeed.

He leaned toward her and lifted a hand to brush a tendril of hair off her soft cheek. "Why not you?" When it was obvious that question didn't satisfy her, he said, "The fact of the matter is you intrigue me, Isabel. And I like it."

A soft flush formed on her cheeks and he smiled at the sight.

"What if we have nothing in common? What if we really don't like each other and we get a divorce anyway? Doing it now would save time."

"What don't you like about me?" he asked, putting her on the spot.

"What?"

"What don't you like about me?"

She opened her mouth but no words emerged. Finally she closed it and licked her lips before trying again.

"You're very bossy."

"I can be," he said, lowering his voice. "But I think you like it when I take control in certain areas."

Her face flushed instantly, and he chuckled, lowering his head to kiss her quickly. "What else?"

He heard her swallow.

"Wh-what happens when you see I'm not pregnant? Will it be over then?"

She attempted to set a time limit as a way to protect herself. His admiration rose. "Mmm." He kissed her again, letting his lips linger over the feel of her. "Then we reevaluate. Arranged marriages have started with less than the chemistry we have, Isabel."

"That's not a mark on the pro side," she said wryly, her nose wrinkling as she pulled away and glanced around to see if anyone watched them. "Looks—and sex drive—fade over time. Those don't sustain a marriage. Not...not the kind I'd like to have."

The kind like her parents and the Babes had. The report had listed the years the group had spent together, with Ms. Georgia and her husband married sixty-five years before the man had passed away.

Everett fought the urge to pick Isabel up and throw her over his shoulder like a caveman. Because unbeknownst to her, she'd just told him exactly what he wanted to hear. He felt the same way. It was yet another thing they had in common. But he sensed by agreeing with her words now, she would think it an attempt to love bomb her or get his way, so he remained quiet. "I understand. So for now we date, bide our time, and see what happens. Are we in agreement?"

The stubborn set of her chin revealed that she

wasn't going to give an inch. But that was okay. The hardest battles brought the best rewards.

"No sex. I shouldn't have... If we're to find out if we're compatible, that has to be off the table."

"If you say so," he readily agreed, leaving it up to her should she change her mind. "Do we have an agreement?"

"I...I suppose."

He gave her one last quick kiss and then took her hand in his. "Let's go," he said, tugging her after him.

"Go where? Everett, where are we going?"

AN HOUR LATER, Everett felt Isabel's hard stare boring into the side of his face. He ignored it and fought off the urge to smile as well.

"What's that?" he asked, pointing toward the structure in the distance.

"It's the Oak Island Lighthouse. Why do you have a driver? Do you not know how to drive? I mean, you are from New York City, so I guess it's understandable if you don't, but I would've thought—"

"I know how to drive." She waited for him to say more, but he fixed his attention on the passing scenery and the beauty surrounding them and purposely ignored her inquisitiveness and focused on her shiver.

The air held the slightest bit of a chill coming off the waterway. "Are you cold?"

Taking the moment for the opportunity it was, he shifted his stance so that his chest met her back. With his arms on either side of her, the scent of her shampoo in his nose, he cuddled her close with his lips next to her ear. "You smell delicious. Coconut and...honey," he guessed. "It makes me want to take a bite out of you."

Everett smiled at the shiver that raced through her body but didn't comment on it. No doubt she would blame the wind cutting across the water as they traveled to Southport, but the statement seemingly distracted her from her questions as to Tomas's presence on board.

"You said no sex," she muttered.

He lowered his head, pressed his lips near her ear. "Holding you isn't sex, Isabel. Nor is touching you, kissing you, or a variety of other things."

Standing over her like he was, he saw her lips part to draw in a breath and smiled, very glad he wasn't the only one so impacted by the chemistry they shared.

The horn sounded as they neared the shoreline, and the captain asked everyone to return to their vehicles. Tomas had remained in the SUV but started to get out when they descended from the upper deck. Everett shook his head and the man remained inside.

He could open Isabel's door. He would protect her with his life. But that didn't mean there weren't people out there who might decide to test his priorities just for the attention it might bring. Which was why a quick text to Tomas had the man waiting for them outside the oceanfront rental, ready to take them on the adventure of the day.

Tomas drove them off the ferry but turned left not long after, stopping at the gate to get a ticket to park at the marina. Their next ferry was a passenger ferry only, and Everett debated whether to have Tomas wait in Southport for their return or accompany them.

Tomas's gaze met Everett's in the rearview mirror, and Everett gave in with a reluctant nod. Better safe than sorry. He might leave Tomas behind on occasion to get some time alone, but he'd never do anything that might endanger Isabel. And the sad truth was that, in today's world, being near him had its own danger, if for no other reason than the threat of kidnapping and ransom.

They'd be on an island without easy access to the mainland should something go wrong. Better to have security and not need it than to find himself without it.

"Oh, I love going to Bald Head," Isabel said when she realized what was happening.

On board the passenger ferry, Isabel chose a seat on the outside so she could see the water yet be behind a bulkhead that blocked them from the worst of the wind after the ferry got underway. Tomas stood nearby at the end, a silent but watchful guard. "You've done this before."

She smiled and shrugged. "Yes, but it never gets old. And it's been years since I've visited even though it's so close."

Isabel nervously rambled on about the various trips she'd taken to the island over the years. They discussed antics she'd played with her sisters in the golf carts and how she and friends had ditched school once to ride bikes to the far side of the island to watch the kite surfers.

He enjoyed the stories. But more than anything he liked watching her expressions as she reminisced. Her childhood was night and day from his, but he liked that she so willingly shared those special moments with him and made him feel a part of them.

Once docked, Isabel led the way to the rental kiosks. Tomas stood in line to get their golf carts while he and Isabel waited off to the side.

"I'm, uh, going to go to the ladies' room before we get going," she said, moving toward the public building several feet away.

Left on his own, Everett shoved his hands into his pockets and strolled around the interior of the building, checking out a map of the island and noting points of interest.

The island had a spaciousness to it Everett

appreciated. It was definitely a retreat for the senses, the lack of traffic noise and the crush of people sliding into his soul like a balm.

"I can't believe my eyes. Everett? Is that you?"

Everett turned to face the man speaking to him, recognizing him instantly. "John. Hello."

John Shapiro grinned and held out a hand to shake.

"I don't believe it! What are you doing here?"

"I could ask you the same."

"I have a house here. My wife's family's from the area, so the wife and I come here for Thanksgiving and fly all the kids down. We gather at our house for the festivities."

"That sounds fun." And like something he'd like to do one day.

"It's the highlight of our year. Are you looking into real estate on the island? I know of a few places for sale. Would be nice to have you as a neighbor."

"Just looking around today," he told the man. "But I'll call to get those names if I decide to move forward."

"John? We're ready," a woman called from somewhere out in the sunshine.

"Looks like they're all loaded up," John said, holding out a hand to shake yet again. "If you're going to be in the area for a while, I hope you'll get in touch. I'll buy you lunch at the club."

"I'd like that. I'll let you know."

The man said his goodbyes and walked out from beneath the building and around the corner. A few seconds later, a six-person golf cart scooted by with a honk of its horn, followed by a second one equally loaded with people, while a third cart loaded with luggage brought up the rear.

Everett watched them go, his thoughts returning to the logistical side of his relationship with Isabel.

He loved New York, the challenge of mastering and excelling in the business world. But this? This was good, too.

If he and Isabel were able to make it work, would she prefer the Carolinas? Maybe split their time between New York and Carolina Cove...or here? Would they be able to come to a compromise that fit both their needs?

You have to win her first.

And that wasn't proving to be easy. Which only made it more fun. He *did* like a challenge.

"You seem deep in thought."

Everett nodded toward the map and lifted a shoulder in a shrug. "It looks like a nice place to live."

"It is. But you need deep, deep pockets to live here. Which reminds me, what do you do again?"

A smile tugged at his lips at the suspicious sound of her voice. "I'm a businessman."

A huff left her and he watched as her expression became uncomfortable. "What? Do you not like entrepreneurs? Are we too boring for an up-and-coming artist?"

"No, it's just you're very evasive."

"I am?" He didn't want to get her suspicions up, but he liked that she seemed to see him just as a man rather than a bank account.

"You are. Which makes me wonder if businessman means...other things."

He watched as she shook her head and bit down on that lower lip so hard he lifted a hand to cup her jaw, using his thumb to save the abused flesh. "What other things?"

"If you're"—her voice lowered—"connected?"

"Connected?"

"You know," she said, exasperation clouding her voice. "In the *mob*?"

The surprised laugh that burst from his chest echoed throughout the open-air enclosure. He used his hold to tug her closer, and her eyes widened as she lifted her hands between them. He ignored the warning and pressed a lingering kiss to her lips, smiling the entire time.

"It wasn't that funny," she said, eyes open on his. "And besides, you didn't answer."

He kissed her again before lifting his head. "No, Isabel, I'm not in the mob. Do you think your cousin would be associated with such people?"

It wasn't uncommon for just about anyone to have some tie to the underworld when it came to the business dealings in New York, but Everett had made it a point to avoid such connections. If there was even a remote chance that Michael...

"No, of course not. I only asked because of *you* and your evasiveness."

"Ready to go, Mr. Drake," Tomas said, joining them.

Tomas handed one of the keys to Everett, but Isabel quickly plucked the key from his palm.

"This way you get to look around more," she said, her smile a bit forced.

Driving also gave her a modicum of control of where they went, and after her mob question, he supposed he didn't mind her insistence. Whatever made her comfortable.

Everett lifted a hand toward the waiting carts. "After you."

CHAPTER EIGHT

H ours later, after a day spent visiting the various beaches on the island, exploring the trails, perusing the gift shops and island market, climbing the lighthouse, and sitting in the peacefulness of the tiny yet gorgeous church, they finished their dinner well after sunset and made their way back to the ferry to return to Southport.

They'd eaten at a restaurant near the marina for convenience's sake, but Jacob had texted various options, including the private club on the far end of the island.

One call to John Shapiro would get them inside, but Everett didn't want the questions that would arise from the ability. Isabel was already suspicious and knew being able to get access to such a private club meant he had strings to pull and the means to do so. It seemed as though she hadn't Googled him yet given her mob question, and he hoped to keep it that way as long as possible.

Her nervous chatter had faded as she'd grown tired, and he tucked her into his side when he saw her stifling a yawn. Over the last hour or so, her guard had finally lowered and she seemed to be more relaxed with him. "Did you have a good day?"

The warm, upward tilt of her lips told him all he needed to know.

"Yeah, I did. Thank you for buying me the sweatshirt. And humoring me when it came to getting the shells and sea glass."

"My pleasure." They looked like typical tourists, both in newly purchased outerwear to combat the evening chill as they ferried back to Southport. The temperature had dropped considerably, changing over from the beautiful eighty-degree day to somewhere in the lower fifties, though it felt cooler on the water. "Isab—"

"Ever—"

Both stopped and waited for the other to continue. "You first," he urged.

She tilted her head back against his upper arm, and he stared down at her beautiful face. The lights on the boat highlighted the angles and planes, the delicate arches of her eyebrows, and the fullness of her lower lip.

"I was just... I've talked all day. Tell me about you. What should I know about you?"

The softly spoken request held the weight of her worries. "What would you like to know?"

"A businessman?"

Smiling, he used his free hand to tuck a wind-tossed curl behind her ear. "Yes. Not a mobster. I began with a few startups after I graduated college, then moved on to takeovers. Some were friendly, some not."

"But nothing illegal, right?"

"Nothing illegal," he said, stroking his finger over her soft cheek.

"I'm guessing you're pretty well-off then, even if you don't act like it. Well, other than having a driver," she mused dryly. "And an assistant who travels with you."

He didn't correct her statement, letting her process things however she wanted. "Is there anything else you'd like to know?"

"Have you been married...before?"

"No. Never."

"I suppose if we weren't *actually* married, then you wouldn't be here."

Once again he didn't comment. But the question did make him stop and wonder.

If the chapel hadn't been fake... If he'd simply met Isabel, they'd had their fun, and then gone their separate ways...

Would he have come to find her? Pursued her as he did now?

The legally binding marriage had definitely added an aspect he hadn't considered, but the truth of the matter was she had thoroughly intrigued him.

Enough to want her regardless of their marital state?

Given his fascination with her, he believed so. No, he *knew* so. But how did he convince her of that?

"Do you have family?"

"My father. And a series of stepsiblings. I'm not close to any of them, though."

"Oh," she said, sounding solemn. "Why not?"

"My father's wives didn't tend to stick around long enough to form attachments."

"That's why you were in Vegas, though. For your father's wedding, right?"

"Yes. Wife number eight."

"*Oh.* Wow."

Oh, wow, indeed. He felt much the same way. Eight marriages. Eight women willing to tie themselves to a man with a track record that proved the odds weren't in her favor.

Statistics stated a first marriage had a fifty-fifty chance of survival. A second marriage, forty-sixty. Third, thirty-seventy. The eighth...

Despite knowing it was his father's wealth that had at least partially attracted the last seven wives, Everett wanted more than that from a woman. From a relationship.

From Isabel.

"What about your mother?"

"She passed when I was eight. Breast cancer."

"Oh, I'm sorry."

"Thanks." That was the one thing he could say about his father, the man had loved his first wife. Those who'd come after?

Everett had to pass it off as a combination of loneliness, the desire to give him a mother figure, alcohol, and the general need to fill the void his mother's absence had left after she'd died.

"If I ask anything too personal, just say so," Isabel said.

"We're married, Isabel. Ask any questions you like."

"Okay... What was she like, your mom?"

He wrapped his arm around Isabel and snuggled her closer, sharing his body heat when he felt her shiver. He should probably insist they go inside the ferry so she'd be warmer, but he liked the sound of the water and the darkness and Isabel huddled at his side.

Rubbing his hand up and down her arm, he considered her question. "She smelled like flowers." It was the first thing that came to mind. "I don't know what kind. She had dark hair, blue eyes. And she laughed. A lot. Even when she was sick. I got a book of jokes at school once and raced home to read them to her. She laughed until she cried."

"Oh, Everett. That's so sweet. I'm sure she

enjoyed every second of those jokes and her time with you."

He kissed the top of her head, his thoughts going back to better days, at least briefly. "I was sent off to boarding school not long after she passed. My father lost himself in grief and immediately began dating a wealthy woman who wanted nothing to do with a child who didn't want anyone but his mother. So off I went."

She inhaled sharply.

"That's *cold*. How could they do that to you?"

"My father said it was for the best, so he could build a new life for us."

Her eyebrows pinched over her nose as she stared up at him, concern written in every line of her face, eyes glassy with tears. "Did you like school? Any of it?"

The fact that she cried for the child he'd been tugged on his heartstrings. "I hated it. I was small for my age and got bullied by the older kids. It made me smarter, though."

"How so?"

He looked away from her to stare through the railings at the water drifting by. "I couldn't beat them physically, so I had to figure out ways to outsmart them. Or hide from them." He chuckled again and squeezed her tighter. "I remember the moment I realized that my bullies didn't like books. The school library became a refuge for me. So much so I wound up sneaking in a pillow and blanket one evening."

"That sounds innocent enough."

"It was. Until they sounded the alarm because the school thought I'd run away."

"Oh, no. What happened? Did you get into trouble?"

"I was sound asleep when they finally checked the locked library. Needless to say, I had some explaining to do."

"Did you tell them about the bullies?"

"No. But I suspected they knew. Still, when I kept my mouth shut, the older boys backed off some."

"Did you go home? For the holidays and summer breaks?"

The lights of Southport twinkled as they neared the marina where the ferry would dock. "A few times. I preferred to stay at school. As much as I hated it and not having friends, it was easier than dealing with whatever wife my father was on and her children."

"They didn't go to boarding school, too?"

The ferry slowed to prepare to dock, and people began to crowd the side where they sat, anxious to debark and get home. "No. They got to stay there."

Everett held on to Isabel as he urged her to stand, noting how well she fit to his side.

"I'd have been your friend."

His entire body clenched at the barely audible whisper, one she probably thought he couldn't hear.

Everett pressed a kiss to the top of Isabel's head and inhaled her scent once again. He thought of the boarding school girls he'd met over the years. Rich, entitled. Unwilling to risk their popularity in any way. Especially with someone they considered the runt of the school. But Isabel...

Everett knew in his gut Isabel would've gone out of her way to make friends with the loner he'd learned to be before his body had grown and changed and turned into the man he now was. Things came easier for him now, but he'd never forget that lost boy and the many lessons he'd learned.

But if he'd had any doubts about keeping Isabel, she'd just sealed her fate with that whisper.

THE MOMENT EVERETT dropped her off outside the lower-level apartment door, Izzy ran upstairs and hurried to uncover her easel, determined to work while inspiration was fresh in her mind.

Today...today had been odd. On the one hand, she'd enjoyed her day with Everett immensely, but on the other hand, fear gripped her heart at the thought of spending the next week or so with Everett because she could easily see herself catching feelings for the man, even though she knew he'd leave once he knew for certain he wasn't going to be a father.

Was love at first sight actually possible?

She didn't think so.

Never had.

If the Babes' marriages had taught her anything, it was that love took time, effort. Commitment. Everyone knew love was a choice, a commitment to stick with someone even when you didn't like them, much less love them. That was the game changer in every relationship.

And finding that level of commitment in today's world was like discovering gold at the bottom of the ocean.

Isabel sat on the edge of her stool and stared at the shadowy outline in front of her. She'd started the painting the day after her return from Vegas, putting brush to paint in the hope of getting Everett out of her head. Now she found her favorite brush, uncovered her oil paints, and took a breath before leaning forward to lose herself in the sound of the brush moving over the textured canvas.

Normally she liked to play music while she painted, but the night's silence suited her mood and allowed her to focus on the details she'd mentally captured and memorized throughout the day. Details missing until now.

The fine lines around his eyes, the deeper wrinkles on his forehead and look in his dark gaze that made her wonder at his thoughts—and yet certain she read them correctly. The details made the painting come alive and her hand trembled in excitement as she raced to capture it all before the memories left her.

The hint of gray just beginning to appear at his temples. The plumpness of his lower lip she'd gotten wrong until now.

Isabel lost herself in creation, working until the wee hours of the morning, all to capture the man who had so quickly taken over her thoughts and dreams.

Strong hands at his sides, a serious expression on his handsome face. The scruff on his jaw, blunt angled chin. Thick eyebrows above the sooty lashes Tessa had found so mysterious.

His face transformed in front of her, and even though it was her hand doing the work, there were moments when Isabel felt as though it belonged to someone else. The minute details kept coming, the shades of flesh, the shadows and hollows of his handsome, craggy face. Everett was one of those men who'd age like fine wine. Or whiskey. Something rich and full-bodied and packed with experiences.

Hours passed before Izzy set the brush aside and stood, stretching arms over her head and not bothering to stifle a loud, mouth-open-and-ugly yawn.

She tilted her head to one side and took a small

step back. Then another. Finally a third, unable to go farther because she bumped into a stack of unpainted canvases behind her. "Wow," she breathed, a shiver rolling over her skin.

She stared at the dark gaze looking back at her and felt her lungs seize. In the last year, she'd grown as an artist. She knew she had, but this...this was proof. This was visceral. Everett stared back at her, looking as though he read her mind and relished the ability to do so.

And even though she didn't like to paint anything she wasn't willing to sell, she knew this one would stay with her forever. She would keep it long after Everett left her behind. A memory of their time together she could hold on to when loneliness over-took her.

Izzy glanced at the clock on her stove and yawned again. Five thirty-four. She'd been at it ever since Everett had dropped her off a little after eleven.

Was it too much to hope he'd have business to attend to this morning? Wouldn't show up at her door at some unholy hour wanting to sightsee?

She lowered her arms and crossed to the couch, grabbing a throw from the chair as she passed by before dropping onto the velvet surface, uncaring of the paint smudges she undoubtedly carried. Practically everything in her apartment was paint-smudged, much to her mother's horror.

Izzy rolled to her side and curled around a

pillow, drowsily blinking at the canvas across the room.

It needed a title.

But so much went into choosing a name.

And how could she name something when she had no idea what—who—it was?

CHAPTER NINE

The days leading up to Thanksgiving passed in a whirlwind.

Everett arrived on her doorstep daily with coffee and then barely gave her time to get dressed before they went exploring. Given her late nights painting, mornings were difficult, and she relied heavily on the caffeine he bribed her with to get moving.

Everett took her for walks on the beach, and he held her hand as the surf rolled over their feet. Every evening they tried a different restaurant, most of which she hadn't been able to afford since losing her parental allowance after dropping out of college. Her earnings paid for the basics and little else, but since painting was all she'd ever wanted to do, she didn't consider it a sacrifice. Nor did she believe her future had to be based off a degree she framed and hung on the wall. Though the irony wasn't lost on her that her paintings were treated the same way.

She'd worked on the various projects she had going before leaving for Las Vegas, but knowing Everett would leave town in a matter of days gave her the excuse she needed to procrastinate and allow herself to enjoy the time she could spend with him.

Every day was a new adventure, and she'd be lying if she said the time off exploring the area she loved didn't go a long way to refill her creative well. Not to mention the company. Everett made their days fun as well as romantic, something that private, secret part of her craved. She might be a bit mouthy on occasion, and Amelia considered her to be "tough," but like most every woman, she'd at least silently admit to needing to feel wanted. A priority.

Loved?

She couldn't speak for Everett, but he was all she thought of when he wasn't around. He consumed her thoughts, her dreams. Even those had taken a turn for the better in that she often relived the night in Vegas and woke hot-cheeked and breathless.

"Did you fall asleep on me?"

She smiled at Everett's deep murmur but didn't open her eyes as Tomas drove them back from Wrightsville Beach and yet another restaurant. If she wasn't careful, she'd gain twenty pounds by the time Everett left Carolina Cove.

The thought of him leaving made her heart

twinge with regret, and she tried to brace herself for what she knew was coming. Maybe for some people it would be easy to just go with the moment and see how things went, but she knew herself well enough to know she wasn't a long-distance type of woman. She wanted it all. Love. Friendship. A marriage like her parents' that withstood the test of time and all the trials life brought.

Izzy nuzzled her face against Everett's jacket-clad shoulder with a shake of her head and a low sound.

"Why so quiet, Isabel?"

The way her name rolled off his lips in his deep voice sent a shiver through her, and she mentally shook her head at herself. "My mother wants me to invite you to Thanksgiving dinner tomorrow," she said, broaching the subject she'd avoided all week.

"And you?"

"And me what?"

"Do you want me to attend?"

Oh, tough question. "You're welcome to come, Everett."

"That's not what I asked."

She bit her lip and avoided looking at him.

"What are you thinking, Isabel? Talk to me."

She shook her head and refused to give voice to the thoughts swirling in her brain.

"Is it perhaps that you're worried you're thinking

about me too much? About us and the future possibilities our relationship holds?"

Unable to stop herself, she lifted her gaze and found him watching her closely.

"Because if that's the case, all I can say is that I feel the same way. I'm thinking of those things, too."

"You are?"

The SUV jolted a bit as Tomas turned onto her street, but it was nothing compared to the jolt his words had given her.

They rolled to a stop outside London's Lattes, and Tomas put the vehicle in park.

Everett got out and held up a hand to help her exit. The gesture was sweet, romantic. And once again, her heart did a little flip of joy she tried and failed to ignore. She was way too easy. Her emotions were overruling her brain and the realistic view she tried to maintain regarding their situation.

Because this? She could see this going badly. Ending badly. For her. Because what woman didn't want to be swept off her feet by a gorgeous man?

If she let Everett lure her into a false sense of security only to pull the rug out from her under when the novelty wore off and he realized she was an emotional, somewhat crazy, and totally territorial woman with insecurity issues that came out in her work as an artist...

By then it would be too late to protect herself from the heartbreak she could so easily see.

Heartbreak.

Like an anchor settling in an ocean, she knew that was the name of the painting drying in her apartment. The one of Everett.

Heartbreak.

How many girlish fantasies began with a gorgeous prince coming to her rescue? But she wasn't a little girl anymore. Times had changed. Men had changed. And a man like Everett? "It's late. I should get some sleep."

"You didn't answer my question," he murmured. "Do you want me to join you for Thanksgiving?"

She swallowed hard and nodded, not because it was rude to say otherwise but because by then she should have her answer to the pregnancy issue, and it might be her last chance to spend time with him once he knew the truth.

She also didn't want him to be alone on Thanksgiving. Her family might be borderline insane at times, but she knew she was loved. And Everett's response to her question about boarding school had tugged at her heartstrings. She didn't want to be like his father and stepmothers. Didn't want to be the person who sent him away so coldly.

How could a child deal with such things?

Was that why he was so insistent now?

How could it not be? Everett knew what it was like to not be wanted, abandoned by a father who ran after other people but not his own child. Everett did everything in his power to be there for the child she might or might not carry, and she couldn't even dislike him for it because it was so sweet.

Her hands fisted, and in that moment, she wished Everett's father was there so she could give him a piece of her mind.

She'd considered Googling Everett on multiple occasions, but every time she grabbed her phone to do just that, she tossed it away out of guilt. But now that she thought about it...how had he known where she lived?

"Pardon?"

Realizing she'd murmured the question aloud as he'd led her across the street, she focused and tried again. "How did you know where I lived? Did you ask Michael?"

A muscle ticked in his jawline, revealed by the streetlamps and building lights above their heads.

"No. When I got back to New York, I did some investigating," he admitted. "My attorney insisted on it after he discovered our marriage."

His attorney. Okay then.

She supposed it made sense, but now their relationship or whatever one would call it felt one-sided. He knew about her, not that there was anything to know, but she was still in the dark about him. She hadn't even stalked him on social media because there was just something creepy about it when she could get it straight from the source. "I see."

"Isabel, you can ask me anything," he said. "I hope you *will* ask if you have questions about me."

"I do have questions. Plenty," she said, her unease at being "investigated" coming to the forefront. "Who are you? Why do you have a driver and an assistant and...and an attorney who tells you to investigate me?"

He lifted his hand and ran it gently over her cheek.

"I think you've already deduced that I am a wealthy man. And their jobs are to project me and my interests."

A huff left her. "I don't want your money, Everett. Do you want me to scream it from the rooftops? Sign something?" She sucked in a sharp gasp. "Oh, my— Does your attorney think us getting married in Las Vegas was deliberate? That I *tricked* you or something?"

Everett didn't believe that. Did he? It was a stupid accident!

But what wealthy businessman wouldn't believe that about someone they didn't know but found themselves shackled to? Was that why he waited to see whether she was pregnant? So he'd have more control over the situation as her husband if she was? So then what? Pay her off? Take the baby? Would he try to take *her* baby?

Over my dead body.

"No, Isabel. I don't believe that."

She stared up at him, trying to rein in her rapid thoughts and the shock and sudden anger that flooded with them. Everett seemed sincere but did she believe him? Could she? "I have to go."

"Isabel—"

"Good night, Everett." She yanked open the downstairs door and paused when he called out to her again.

"Isabel, what's going on? I don't want to fight with you."

"I don't want to fight either." She inhaled and forced herself to breathe. "Be at my parents' house at eleven."

"I'll pick you up."

She shook her head firmly back and forth. "No. I'll meet you there. That way they'll not get the wrong idea. It's better that way."

Better for them.

And better for her so that *she* didn't get the wrong idea?

———

NINE O'CLOCK THE NEXT MORNING, a knock sounded at her door and Isabel groaned.

"I hear you in there," Everett said, a smile in his voice.

The deep rumble warmed her heart even though she warned herself away from thinking such things.

His presence was a temporary situation. *And don't you forget that.* "I told you to meet me at my parents' house," she called with a grimace as she sat up on the couch.

"I decided to come here instead," he said, his voice muffled by the door.

Of course he had. Not only had he come here but he'd also come early.

She pushed the blanket and heating pad aside and forced herself to her feet, slogging over to the door to unlock and yank it open.

She gave him a tired glance and leaned heavily against the doorknob.

"Isabel? Did you sleep at all?" he asked, his gaze searching her face with concern.

She could only imagine how bad she looked after a night of bingeing *Buffy the Vampire Slayer.* "Not much," she said, avoiding his gaze and turning to trudge back across the floor.

"What's going on?"

"I googled you." Because in the middle of the night, when her stomach was getting ripped to shreds by period cramps, what else was there to do? If Buffy had had the internet, she wouldn't have had to go to the library and depend on Giles so much for information.

"I see."

She shot a look at Everett over her shoulder and saw him gently close her door. Biting her lip, she plucked the cozy blanket off the couch and wrapped it around her before plopping down on the couch once more. "Good news, Mr. Billionaire. I'm not pregnant."

"You took a test?"

"Don't need to," she stated pointedly. "So you and your attorney can breathe easy and get the divorce papers ready. Now I get why you were both so nervous. No prenup. Good thing I'm not a gold digger."

He stood over her, hands on his lean hips as he watched her. She flushed under his scrutiny and noted the way he took in the bottle of pain relievers on the coffee table as well as the heating pad.

"You're hurting."

"Nothing I haven't dealt with all of my life." Sensing his displeasure, she shrugged. "Endometriosis. The first day or two is always the worst, then it lets up."

He took off his suit jacket and tossed it over a nearby chair.

"Did you tell your family you won't be coming?"

She rolled her head on the pillow and stared at him through drowsy eyes. "Not yet."

Everett took out his phone and she watched as he typed. "What are you doing?"

"Texting Michael."

"What? No."

"Yes," Everett said, not looking up from the

screen. "The last thing you need is the stress of a family gathering where everyone is watching us. We'll spend Thanksgiving Day here."

"We?"

Done texting, he slipped the phone back into his pocket and headed toward the bathroom. Isabel gave up on trying to get him out of her apartment and listened as he turned on the taps and began filling the tub.

Finding out her handsome Vegas crush was a real-life billionaire had been eye-opening. And while Everett was gorgeous and funny and intelligent all on his own, his money made her insanely nervous rather than excited at the thought of being a billion-aire's wife.

Everett emerged and she noted he'd rolled up his shirt sleeves. The sight of his strong hands and hairy forearms drew her attention. How sad was it that even his arms were sexy? "Thanks for the bath. You can go."

He didn't say anything as he lightly gripped her elbow and pulled her upright on the couch before slipping his other arm under her knees and plucking her up. "What are you doing?"

"Pampering you."

"Everett—"

"You're wasting energy you don't look like you have by arguing with me, Isabel." He carried her through the doorway to the bathroom and sat her on the closed toilet seat.

She looked around and realized he'd already pulled towels from the linen closet to have at the ready, had poured her favorite shower gel into the tub, and seemed to have every intention of pampering her like he said.

"Strip and get in. I'll fix you some breakfast."

"This isn't necessary." She pushed her fingers through her hair in a huff. "I'm not pregnant. Or hungry. You can stop pretending you want to be here and go back to New York."

She'd stared down at her bare toes and chipped polish when she'd made the statement, but the next second, she found his hand under her chin, lifting, and his gaze steady on hers.

"Isabel..."

"What?"

He searched her gaze for such a long, silent moment that her breathing turned shallow.

"Who's pretending?"

CHAPTER TEN

W hat are you working on? May I see it?"
Everett asked a half hour later.

She'd soaked in the tub until the water started to cool and then hurried to get out and dressed when she remembered the fact Everett was in her apartment with the draped painting of himself.

Would he peek to see what was under the covering? Respect her privacy?

His question was her answer, and her toes curled into the carpet in response. Honorable men were hard to come by, and had he peeked, he wouldn't have been the first to ignore her request to do whatever they wanted. "It's... I don't like showing my work until I'm ready." Her face felt hot when she swiped a hand over her cheek to dislodge a hair tickling her mouth.

She had multiple paintings scattered all over her apartment, but that was the only one that was draped. Isabel left the island stool where she'd sat finishing up the toast and egg he'd fixed for her breakfast and returned to the couch.

She'd no sooner sat down than Everett joined her, physically shifting her so that he sat behind her. Once she settled, his large hands descended on her shoulders and gently rubbed. With a low gasp, she moaned as he pressed and massaged the tight muscles.

"That is a sound I'd like to hear more of," he murmured into her ear.

Her body hummed as though from a surge of electricity, and an embarrassed laugh huffed from her chest. "I think we both know that's not a good idea."

She sank her teeth into her lower lip and bit down hard when he found a particularly tight spot, scrunching her face up in an effort to stay silent when it felt like her bones and muscles melted at his touch.

"I disagree. I remember it as a very good idea."

Still in la-la-Everett-land, she shrugged. He could disagree all he liked but it didn't change facts.

"Lean back."

"You're very bossy," she said, sliding a glare at him and then wishing she hadn't. Why did the man have to look so good? Appeal in so many ways? Take care of her? She loved getting pampered. She wasn't sure what love language pampering fell under, but it was definitely hers. Cuddling, hair stroking, back rubs. It was a struggle not to purr when he did those things.

Eyes closed, she let Everett have his way, reminding herself that their situation was temporary.

It would be a whole lot easier if Everett was an unattractive, uncaring bore. But he wasn't. And with every touch and squeeze and brush of his fingertips, she fell deeper under his spell.

"Isabel, we need to talk."

"Uh-uh. Nothing good ever comes from those words."

He chuckled at her mumbling, grumbling tone, but the gentle squeeze of her shoulders told her he meant business.

"I want you to come to New York with me."

Her entire body froze. "What?"

With one last squeeze of her shoulders, he gently pushed her forward before pressing her back to the couch so that she faced him.

"I want you," he said softly, staring deeply into her eyes, "to come to New York with me."

The first three little words and the heat in his gaze sent a shiver through her before the rest of them resonated. He wasn't joking. "To New York?" She repeated the words in a desperate bid to get her brain to work.

"Yes."

"But...Everett, I'm *not* pregnant. We can get the divorce now. Give me the papers and I'll sign them. I'm sure your attorney has probably drawn them up already." A muscle ticked in his jaw, and she tilted her head to one side. "Am I right?"

"He did, not because I asked him to, and not to my satisfaction," he added without further explanation.

He seemed to think the clarification was important, and maybe it was to him, but for her? "What was it you told me? Their job is to look out for your best interests? I'm sure he's anxious to get you out of the mess we created...." Her words trailed off because obviously Everett's best interests did not lie with her.

He lifted his hand and gently cupped her chin, rubbing his thumb over her lips.

"I want to give you a Christmas present."

"Oh, Everett, that's not—"

"I wanted to surprise you, but since you're fighting me on this, I suppose I'll tell you. I took the liberty of sending photos of your work to a few acquaintances. They would like to meet with you in person. Before the holidays."

She swallowed hard. Wait, what? "Acquaintances?" she asked, needing the clarification.

"Gallery owners, curators."

From the New York art world? Shock rolled through her. She'd never been able to get any attention there. So much of the world was based on who a person knew and the networks around them. Locally she did okay, but wasn't it every artist's dream to see their work on gallery walls the world over? "Why... why would you do that?"

"Why wouldn't I do that for you?" he asked instead.

"I don't... I mean, I-I dunno. I don't know what to say. I'm just surprised." Flabbergasted was more like it. Shocked. Blown away. Her last boyfriend had been jealous of the time she spent painting. He'd wanted her to sit beside him on the couch and watch him play video games instead. He'd complained that she smelled of paint thinner and oil paints and always wanted to go to boring museums and galleries.

But Everett...supported her art? Wanted to help her. "Why?" she asked softly again.

He looked decidedly uncomfortable for a moment before slowly releasing her after one last gentle swipe of his thumb over her mouth.

"Because if I can help you, I want to."

"What's the catch?"

"No catch."

"*Everett.*" She sensed his frustration with her growing but ignored it for the answers she sought.

"Fine. If you have to have a catch, I suppose it's the fact that, while we're there, I'm hoping you'll attend some events with me."

"What kind of events?"

"Parties and gatherings. Maybe a gala or two. It's the holidays," he said as though that would explain everything.

She supposed it did. Her attorney father certainly had had his share of invitations to various functions over the years, and he was nowhere near Everett's level of wealth. "Galas?"

His mouth curled up at the corners and her pulse picked up speed.

"Are you going to be stubborn about this?"

She smiled at his teasing. "I wouldn't be me if I wasn't."

"Say yes, Isabel. You can have your meetings and tour the galleries, I'll have a stunningly beautiful date for events I'd rather ignore, and while we're there, we can also enjoy all the festivities of Christmas in New York."

"It sounds...lovely." It wasn't a lie. It sounded like a Hallmark movie or a fairy tale. One she'd love to live. If only for a little while. "What about us?" she forced herself to ask.

He held her gaze, the look in his eyes one she couldn't make out.

"I'm hoping the time there will help us come to an acceptable compromise."

"What kind of compromise? We just need to sign some papers, Everett." His silence and narrowed gaze left her shaking her head. Now who was being stubborn? "I'm certain your attorney agrees."

"I don't care if he does."

"But...why? The longer we take to get this settled, the more likely it is that my family might find out."

His gaze glittered. "Let them."

"What?"

"Is it so surprising to you that I like you, Isabel? That I'd like to see where this could take us?"

"Are you sure you're not just embarrassed that billionaire Everett Drake mistakenly got married? Everett, you seem like a great guy, but people 'in like' don't get married. Nor does like keep them married. It takes more."

"Maybe we can find more in time."

"How much time? What if we can't? Is this about us not having a prenup? I don't want your money, Everett."

"I believe you. But believing you makes me want this to work even more. I've been honest about not wanting a divorce all along, Isabel."

Everett had been painfully honest from the beginning but...she wasn't sure what she'd thought. Maybe that he'd change his mind. Or lose interest. Especially once he knew there wasn't a baby involved.

Rationally, she knew he was right in thinking there were couples out there with less in common than they had, but it didn't mean she wanted to be one of them, struggling to hold a marriage together that had begun as a prank in the first place. It was only a matter of time until it fizzled. And more than anything, she'd like to think they could end things on good terms and still be friends rather than angry and upset because...

"Take a chance, Isabel. Come with me. See what happens. You never know, you might have fun."

"The last time we had that much fun, we wound up accidentally married."

"Good thing that can't happen again then, huh?"

He lifted his hand and framed her jaw, the heat of his touch calling to a place buried deep within her.

"Let me treat you to New York in style. It's the least I can do since I'm the one who opened the wrong door in Vegas." He tilted his head to one side as he waited for her answer. "Say yes."

She could practically hear her mother shrieking and clapping with glee. Amelia, too. But more than anything, she heard her inner Izzy laugh-crying at the turn of events and the awareness of just how badly her Vegas adventure could have turned out... versus the man before her. "Okay."

"Yeah?"

"Yeah, I'll go. Thank you." His grin warmed her insides to a lava-like degree, and she shifted uncomfortably. "You'll have to let me know exactly what kind of events so I can borrow some outfits off of Amelia."

"I'll take you shopping."

"No. It's fine." The image from *Pretty Woman* flashed into her head, and Isabel immediately shook her head. She didn't want him spending money on her. Not like that. No matter how rich he was.

When Everett woke up and realized some things couldn't end happily, she didn't want him thinking she'd used him in any way. His connections for her agreement to accompany him was a fair trade. After all, her work would have to do the rest, though he'd gotten her foot in the door. "Amelia has a ton of stuff for all the premieres she's invited to, and seeing how she's very pregnant, she's not using any of them. She won't mind."

He didn't look pleased by her refusal of the additional gift but accepted it as though he knew not to push too much.

"Whatever you prefer. Now, how about you go nap while I clean up the kitchen?"

"You're going to clean?"

"I do know how to scrub a pan, Isabel."

"How do I know you won't peek at my work while I'm asleep?" The moment the question left her, she knew she'd said too much. He'd seemed okay with her statement earlier, but now that she'd brought it up again...

Everett lifted his other hand to her face to gently cup and gave her an inquisitive look.

"Are you hiding something, Isabel?"

More than you'll ever know. "I don't like people

looking before I'm finished with a project. Because if you do, I-I can't finish it," she said, hoping God would forgive her the fib. "It's like it loses all of its energy and I-I have to set it aside."

"Well, I wouldn't want to be accused of ruining your next piece. You have my word, I won't look at it. But I hope I'm the first to see it when you've finished."

She gave him a tentative smile but made no promises.

Everett seemed to notice, so when the smile didn't work, she shifted forward to press her lips to his. She felt his moment of surprise that she'd willingly offered a kiss but didn't let it stop her. She needed to see if their chemistry was real. Not just a figment of her imagination or a fun time in Vegas clouded by champagne bubbles.

Not just the fantasy of a handsome billionaire and the thought of the holidays and trip to come.

This was a kiss for her.

By the time she ended the kiss and withdrew, Isabel sucked in a much needed breath and knew she was in trouble. Yeah, chemistry was not a problem. "No peeking," she ordered huskily before ducking around him to rush into her bedroom, shutting the door behind her to hide her flushed cheeks and rapid breaths.

She leaned against the hard paneled wood, desperate to put a lock on the Pandora's box she'd just opened when she thought of them in New York without the prying eyes of her family and friends.

This man...

A stranger.

Didn't feel like a stranger at all.

THE FOLLOWING AFTERNOON, Everett walked into the bar in Carolina Beach and made his way up the stairs to the outside seating, Tomas and Jacob at his heels. Tomas would make himself comfortable within sight of him, while Jacob would join the scheduled planning meeting with Michael so that he could stay informed and up to date on changes.

"Hey," Michael said by way of greeting. "Looks like Carolina Cove agrees with you."

Everett smiled at the words but didn't comment. He shook hands with Michael and then got comfortable, easy to do when he wasn't stuffed into a three-piece suit and strangled by a tie. He rather liked the casualness of this meeting.

Michael had already spread out the plans he worked on, and Everett scanned the paper in front of them. "It's coming along nicely."

"I think so. I incorporated the changes you asked you for last time, as well as a few updates to meet new code. I'll send the digital files to you as well as let you have this copy, and we can schedule to meet up again after you've taken a last look."

"Sounds like a plan. I don't see anything off the bat, but I want to take my time."

"Of course. So...how's things going with you and Izzy?"

He'd known Isabel's cousin would ask about them, but he wasn't sure how much Isabel would want him to share. "Fine. She's coming to New York with me to meet with a couple of galleries."

Jacob's phone rang, and with a look at the face, he excused himself from the table.

"Your doing?"

"I made some inquiries on her behalf. Her work did the rest. She's very talented."

"I agree," Michael said as he lifted his water glass for a drink. "But is that the type of thing you should be doing if you're divorcing? I mean, if it ever becomes public, will those connections withdraw their support because you are no longer involved *on her behalf?*"

He hadn't thought of it that way. "It'll be fine." Especially since he hoped the divorce would never go through. Maybe he was crazy to think they could make a marriage work, but he'd never met anyone like Isabel. Never been as drawn or entertained or fascinated by someone. If that wasn't incentive to try to keep them tied to one another, what was?

"Everett, Izzy isn't...Izzy isn't as worldly as you."

"It's part of her charm," Everett stated honestly. Until Isabel, women seemed to fall into two categories. The trophy-wife wannabe like his father inevitably married or the high-powered career woman with no interest in stepping back in order to have a family and a life outside an office building. He appreciated that women had to make their own decisions when it came to the paths they were willing to take, but that didn't mean he wanted to veer from his own.

No, that meant finding someone with a career path different from his own that could accommodate such a thing. Which, he mused silently, was another point in Isabel's favor.

"It also makes her more vulnerable than you might think."

The waitress brought the drink he'd ordered, and Everett thanked her, waiting for her to walk away before meeting Michael's gaze. "The last thing I want to do is hurt her. Your friendship makes that goal even more important."

Michael seemed to accept his words, but Everett could still read the doubt in his friend's expression.

"So New York is what? A chance to get her to change her mind?" Michael asked.

"If I'm lucky." Everett felt the weight of Michael's gaze and his surprise.

"You really want this to work out, don't you?"

Everett wiped his thumb over the bit of condensation on his glass and decided to be honest. "Isabel has something. Something no other woman has possessed. And I'm now of an age where I think about the future and why I work as hard as I do. This seems to be the next step."

"Does Izzy know that?"

"We haven't discussed things beyond New York. Right now she's focused on the fact we've only known each other a matter of weeks and doesn't believe a future is possible. I thought maybe showing her what our life could be like might help."

"Let's say it does. What then?"

Everett pondered the question...and couldn't stop the smile that formed.

THAT EVENING TESSA pressed her nose to the lavender bouquet delivered to her salon earlier that afternoon and breathed deeply. Had she mentioned how much she loved lavender?

"What have we here?"

Tessa blinked and opened her eyes to find Mary Elizabeth standing just inside the salon door, still holding the knob.

"And I'll also ask *who* has put that smile on your face?"

Tessa flushed but hesitated to tell her friend about Kirk.

"Oh, my word...are they from Bruce?"

"What? *No*. No, I haven't... Why would my ex send me flowers?" Tessa turned away from the bouquet and set about her daily closing routine. Most of the girls had already gone for the day, but a few remained in the kitchen discussing an upcoming concert.

"I just thought since you mentioned seeing him so much—"

"In *passing*. Not in a we've-had-words kind of way." Tessa grabbed a bottle of disinfectant from the cabinet as well as a rag and began spraying down the checkout desk and glass display.

"Okay, but the flowers are from a man?" Mary Elizabeth asked.

"They might be," Tessa said, scrubbing the smudged glass extra hard.

"Tell me everything," MeMe ordered. "What's his name? What does he do? Is he retired? Does he have children?"

Tessa laughed at the barrage of questions, but at the same time, unease settled deep within her. "He's...a businessman."

"A local?"

"Yes, though newish to the area."

"Okay, and...? Come on, why are you being so secretive? It's me!"

"I know, it's just... He's a bit younger than me."

Mary Elizabeth's gaze narrowed suspiciously.

"How much younger?"

Oh, why did her friends *have* to know details? "He'll... be fifty in another month."

Mary Elizabeth gasped and then choked to the point Tessa had to pound her friend on her back before rushing to get a tiny bottle of water from the fridge. Or maybe she should open a bottle of wine now that she'd spilled her news? They literally were on island time.

She shook her head at her musings and twisted off the cap before handing the bottle to Mary Elizabeth, then made the second trip to the fridge. Since salons were safe havens for women the world over, she kept a well-stocked wine selection for just such discussions. "White or red?"

"Your choice," Mary Elizabeth said in a watery-sounding voice. "Tessa...he's *how* many years younger?"

"Are you really going to make me say it? Now you know why I've been so quiet about meeting him. If your reaction is this bad, can you imagine what Cheryl will say?"

Of all the Babes, Cheryl was perhaps the most judgmental and quick to try to keep her family and friends from making what she deemed were mistakes. Cheryl's heart was in the right place, which was why she was forgiven when she got judgy. It just didn't make her comments more palatable.

"It's just that's *young*, even for you."

"What do you mean, even for me?"

"Now don't be that way. You're the one out of all us who's had the most experience with dating. That's all I meant."

Yeah, she got that. When you married your high school crush only to divorce and then buried husbands number two *and* three, it gave you life experience her married forever friends didn't have except by living vicariously through her. "I know. But he doesn't seem too young. He's an old soul."

"Uh-huh. How serious is it between you and this old soul?" MeMe asked.

"We've gone out a few times."

"And you haven't said anything?"

"Why would I when I know just how vocal the Babes will be? Besides, he's a gentleman."

"With a mama fetish."

"I'm not *that* much older. Thirteen years and...eleven months, give or take." *Old enough to be his mama.*

And to appreciate that she wasn't.

"How did you meet?"

Carrying two glasses and the now open bottle, Tessa retraced her steps to where Mary Elizabeth sat and handed her a glass. "We met on the boardwalk. He said he saw me and...had to say hello."

Tessa glanced at Mary Elizabeth's face and tried to read her thoughts. "What? First you ask all kinds of questions and now you're quiet? Say something."

"I'm not... I don't know what to say, to be honest. I know you're lonely and have been wanting to meet someone, but that's quite a lot of difference."

Tessa took a sip of the wine and relished the flavor exploding across her tongue. "No one would think twice if I were a man dating a woman that age."

"Because women are more mature."

"It's *because* there's such a double standard."

Mary Elizabeth sipped her wine, the water bottle now set aside for something more fortifying. "That may be true. But facts are facts and men mature more slowly than women."

"Well, he's still a grown man. We're not talking teenagers here. Or even twentysomethings."

"That's true. So, when do we get to meet this man? What's his name?"

"Kirk. Kirk Delucca."

"Have you googled him?"

"What? No," Tessa said. "Why would I?"

"Because that's the first thing you do in today's dating world. To make sure he's not a serial killer or something."

"Something you learned from your girls?" Tessa asked.

Mary Elizabeth shrugged. "Sophia has been known to have a good head on her shoulders. If she says it's wise to do, it is. He might have a prison record, be an abuser. You just never know."

"*Or* he could just be a nice man who likes older women. As he says, we're...uncomplicated."

"What's that mean?" Mary Elizabeth asked, taking another sip.

Tessa settled into the chair across from her friend and got comfortable since Mary Elizabeth had some time left before she needed to return home. She came to visit every week since Adam had a standing golf game with a judge. "It means we're just dating and having fun."

"Sex?"

Tessa felt her cheeks color like a schoolgirl, but she couldn't help it. "Not just yet. Like I said, he's a gentleman. We're in no rush."

Tessa glanced at her friend and saw her frowning and debated whether she ought to have kept her mouth shut and not revealed her relationship with Kirk just yet. But she'd been dying to talk to someone about it, and it wasn't something she felt comfortable discussing with her adult children.

But if Mary Elizabeth struggled to cope with the news...it didn't bode well for how the rest of the Babes would take it. "Has Isabel heard anything else about her show? Did she get any more sales from it?"

"Changing the subject won't keep me from asking questions."

"We'll get back to it, I'm sure," Tessa murmured. "Her new beau certainly seems taken with her."

MeMe shot Tessa a quelling glare before

nodding. "He does. Michael speaks highly of Everett, too."

"Does that mean you haven't googled him?"

Mary Elizabeth laughed at the question and warily acknowledge Tessa's dig with a shake of her head.

"Fine. You got me. No, I haven't. Michael vouches for Everett. They've been friends for years, so I didn't feel the need."

"But you're worried."

"I...I see his interest in her, and I don't want her to mess things up because she's so determined to go her own way."

"You still don't think Isabel can make it as an artist?"

MeMe groaned and slumped back in the raised salon chair, taking two huge gulps of wine before answering.

"It's not that she's not talented. I *know* she is. I see it. But her art is not everyone's taste, and I hate to see her struggle so much just to make a few sales here and there that only give her hope for more but not a seemingly healthy income."

"Maybe the right people just haven't seen her paintings yet."

"I know but she's thirty-two," Mary Elizabeth stated. "How much longer is she going to chase a dream like a child?"

"Oh, Mary Elizabeth. Be careful there, honey.

That girl has only ever wanted to be an artist. If she hears you saying that..."

"I know. I don't want to hurt her, but she needs to make a living, not just scrape by. What about the future?"

"That's in God's hands, don't you think?" Tessa pointed out.

"Yes, but...I think even He wants us to do what we can to help ourselves."

"She's using her talent. I'd say that counts."

Mary Elizabeth sat pensively a long moment.

"I'd hoped the last-minute invitation to the Las Vegas show would be a milestone and give her the boost she needs, but what if it gave her Everett instead? Hmm? Maybe it's time to refocus on her priorities."

"A man isn't a career, MeMe. The last thing she needs is to fall in love with the wrong man and have him derail her life."

That's what she'd done. She'd fallen. Hard. But the man she'd loved and the one who'd returned from Vietnam were two wholly different people. That man had devastated her and their son.

Mary Elizabeth continued to vent her concerns, knowing she was safe in doing so and it wouldn't be repeated. No mother wanted her child to barely exist. But Izzy was born an artist, and Tessa had a feeling the young woman would never give up so long as she breathed. "Just be careful," she advised once Mary Elizabeth slowed her rant. "Your relationship with Izzy is already strained as it is. Telling her to give up her dream isn't going to make things better between the two of you."

Mary Elizabeth drained the last of her wine and held it out for a refill.

"I know. Just pray that she sees in Everett what I do. He could make her happy."

Tessa held the bottle over MeMe's glass but hesitated a moment before pouring. "Happiness is subjective, MeMe. Your happiness isn't hers."

The chime on the back exit sounded, and Tessa knew the girls had left the kitchen by the calls of goodbye.

"How did you get to be so smart?"

A low chuckle left Tessa and she held up a finger. "That's easy. Forty years of listening to crazed mamas talk to me while in my chair about how their kids are behaving and then getting the updates on their next visits. You can't help but pick up a few parenting tips along the way having heard so many of the end results."

Mary Elizabeth stared down into the depths of her wine, lips pursed as she pondered Tessa's words.

"Can we meet him soon? Your Kirk? You can come for dinner."

"Oh, MeMe, I'm not sure I'm ready for that just yet."

"Just us. Please, Tessa? I want to meet him. To know you'll be safe."

"I could just find someone who'd vouch for him. That might be easier than sitting through a dinner with you interrogating him."

Mary Elizabeth stretched out her free hand and patted Tessa's arm.

"I support you, Tessa. You know that. I just want you to be careful."

"I am. I will be. We're just getting to know one another for now."

"And when he presses for more? Men that age seem to think they have something to prove. They don't call it midlife crisis for nothing."

"I know. And I don't know yet." There would be plenty of time for more later if Kirk stuck around. But for now, his attention and company went a long way in comforting her, distracting her from the emptiness she'd felt since her husband's passing.

A low sound left Mary Elizabeth, and Tessa lifted an eyebrow in question. "What?"

"Oh, nothing. I just wondered if this qualifies you as a cougar?"

"Ha ha."

"No, really! With that kind of age difference, there has to be a name for it," Mary Elizabeth teased. "Tell me more about Kirk Delucca. His name sounds Italian? Is he handsome?"

CHAPTER ELEVEN

W ait, so you're going to New York with him?" Amelia asked, her voice revealing her excitement.

"Yeah. I don't exactly want to turn down the opportunity to meet with the galleries, no matter how it came about," Izzy told her best friend, wrapping her arms around her to hug. "And hello to you, too."

Amelia laughed, her baby belly making the hug awkward as she pulled Izzy across the threshold.

"I'd forgotten about your security. I felt like I was smuggling something in even though I wasn't," Izzy said, referring to the guarded gate at the end of Amelia's street.

"Oh, yeah. Oliver and Marsali both needed security after they moved here, and it just made sense to set it up that way what with Marsali's brother next door and Lincoln and Carter willing to put up with it to keep out the crazies. You'd be surprised how many people do not respect boundaries."

Amelia curled her arm through Izzy's for the walk upstairs, but when they made it to the top, Amelia tugged her to a spare bedroom down the hallway instead of the master.

"I've got everything already set up."

"What's that mean?" Isabel asked.

Amelia flung open the bedroom door, and Izzy gasped before laughing. "Did you leave anything *in* the closet?"

There were clothes everywhere. Tossed over the bed, hanging on a rolling rack. Not just clothes but shoes and boots and purses and wraps. And Marsali. "Oh! Hi, I didn't know you were."

"I told Marsali about your trip, and she asked if she could join the fun," Amelia said.

"I hope you don't mind," Marsali said.

"Not at all."

"Good, because I didn't plan to leave," the woman said with a wide grin. "And I also brought some clothes I thought you might like to try. Oliver and I went to New York a few weeks ago for interviews, and I did a little shopping while there."

Izzy glanced at Amelia, struggling to find the words. "I-I can't thank you enough for the offer but—"

"No buts," Marsali said. "If you like it, borrow it, if not, don't. It's that simple."

"She means it," Amelia said. "Besides, it's winter in New York and you need to look the part. I get why you didn't want to accept Everett's offer of a shopping spree—"

"Smart move," Marsali added in her firm, matchmaker voice.

"So we've got you covered. Besides, I won't be wearing any of this stuff until next winter, if then. Come on and I'll show you."

Amelia pulled Izzy deeper into the room and shut the door behind them.

"Formal gowns are hanging here. Cocktail gowns here. Marsali and I also grabbed some things I thought might work for meetings with the gallery people or just a day on the town. And some casual stuff, too. Oh, this is fun," Amelia said, her eyes twinkling as she guided her burgeoning body down into a chair across the room.

"Fashion show," Amelia ordered. "Hop to it. We want to see everything."

"This is payback for setting you up with Marsali, isn't it?" Izzy teased, nodding her head toward Marsali the matchmaker while grinning.

"Ha," Marsali said, eyeing Amelia. "Be careful how you answer that."

"Considering how well things turned out, what do you think?" Amelia shook her head with a sweet smile, hands cradling her belly. "I wouldn't have Lincoln or my babies."

Twins. How was it possible that, in a short amount of time, her best friend was going to have not one but two babies?

Her mind immediately pictured a dark-haired baby with dark brown eyes, an impish grin, and heart-stopping dimples. Tiny little fingers and toes.

"Earth to Izzy? Hello?"

She blinked at Marsali's voice and rolled her eyes. "Sorry. Just thinking. What should I try first?"

"Casual to formal," Amelia ordered from her chair. "That way we see the progression."

"If you say so."

"When are you leaving for New York?" Marsali asked.

Izzy stared down at the luxurious cashmere sweater dress paired with flesh-colored leggings that had the look of black tights over skin, and above-the-knee boots. That was some serious layering. And for a warm-weather girl, totally necessary to combat the cold. She was thankful her friends knew these things ahead of time. "Um, Sunday. He mentioned going Sunday evening."

In short order, she had everything on and zipped up the boots after leaning against the bed to pull them on. She straightened and walked to the floor-length mirror. The outfit was stunning. She looked professional and...

"Sexy but understated. He'll *love* it," Marsali said with an approving nod.

"Do I want to be sexy?" she asked while meeting Amelia's watchful gaze in the mirror. "I mean, Everett and I are just...friends."

"Are you going to tell her or do I have to break the news to her?" Amelia said to Marsali.

"Tell me what?" Izzy asked.

Marsali stood and moved closer to add a wrap to her shoulders to finish the look. One peek at the mirror and she knew this one was a must pack.

"That men like Everett don't do things like this... unless he's really into you, Izzy. Now the question is, how much do you like him?"

Izzy shifted her gaze from Marsali to Amelia and found her friend staring at her with a searching expression.

"You know," Amelia said softly, "it occurs to me that maybe Marsali should be allowed in on your little secret."

"Secret? What secret?"

Marsali's full attention and excitement left Izzy fumbling for words. She'd told Amelia in confidence, and while Marsali had a seriously fantastic knack for matchmaking, the more people who knew what had happened in Vegas, the more likely it was to get out. "Um..."

"Oh. It's okay. You don't have to tell me if you don't want to," Marsali said. "But believe me when I say I'm the gatekeeper of secrets. Anything you tell me will not be shared. Otherwise I wouldn't have clients," she said with a wink.

"You can trust her, Iz. And Marsali might be able to help you," Amelia stated, hands patting her belly. "She's really good."

"Tell you what," Marsali said, "think about it while you take that off and try the next one."

In short order, Izzy found herself stripping down and trying a pair of black slacks with a black top and camel-colored topcoat. It looked sleek and sophisticated but was comfortable, too.

"That's another yes," Marsali said with a firm nod. "You're two for two, girl."

Unable to stand it any longer, Izzy handed off the coat and pulled the top over her head while Marsali prepped outfit number three. "Everett and I accidentally got married in Vegas."

A bomb going off couldn't have created as much impact as her words.

"I'm sorry, what?" Marsali asked. "Did you just say—"

"Yup."

"She so did," Amelia added, her voice laced with amusement as she watched Marsali's reaction.

Marsali delicately cleared her throat and tilted her head to one side.

"Just how does one go about *accidentally* getting married?"

Izzy explained as quickly and coherently as she could only to watch Marsali lower herself to the edge of the bed like she'd gotten weak in the knees.

"Wow. And now you're..."

"Just friends," Izzy said.

"She wishes they were just friends," Amelia added. "The chemistry between them is hot. And Everett," Amelia said, drawing out his name, "wants to *stay* married."

"Oh. *Oh*," Marsali said, eyes widening. "So this trip is—"

"His way of romancing her into giving up on getting a divorce and agreeing to stick around? That'd be my guess," Amelia said with a wide smile as she crossed her arms atop her belly and gave Izzy a satisfied grin.

"You don't know that," Izzy argued, voice muffled as she pulled a sweater over her head. "It could be a-a goodbye gesture."

Marsali rose from where she'd leaned against the side of the bed and walked toward Izzy.

Izzy faltered beneath her friend's steady stare and fought off the confirmation she saw in Marsali's gaze. "You're wrong."

"I'm not wrong," Marsali said softly. "But I wonder...why are you fighting this so hard? Do you like him?"

"Yes, but—"

"But what?"

Izzy swallowed hard and tried to formulate the words. She knew how it would sound if she said the words aloud. Knew they'd probably laugh and roll their eyes and tell her she was being silly. But she wasn't. She *felt* this way for a reason, and she didn't want to be made fun of because of it.

"Iz?" Amelia hefted herself to her feet and waddled over to where they stood.

Izzy clutched the short leather skirt in her hand and wished...she just wished she could make sense of it all. "What do I have to offer him? I mean, he's... I think it's pretty obvious he's wealthy," she said, avoiding the part about googling him. "But he's also smart. He's...he's the whole package."

"So are you," Marsali said, her pinched features revealing the seriousness of her.

"No, not like that. I don't own anything except for Betty. I barely get by, and saying I'm an artist can be loosely interpreted as me begging people to allow me to place something in their stores on the off chance it might sell."

"But you have sold your art. You've sold lots of it," Amelia said.

"Not enough," Izzy said.

"So maybe you haven't hit it big but you will. It's coming," Amelia said.

"And success isn't just about money. It's living how you want to live," Marsali added. "As to what you have to offer, Everett obviously sees more in you than *you* see in you."

"It's just painfully obvious he's out of my league."

Marsali clicked her tongue and placed her hands on Izzy's shoulders, using her hold to spin her around to face the mirror once again.

"What do you see?" Marsali asked.

"I see a thirty-two-year-old woman with a bad dating history."

Marsali chuckled and shook her head. "You are stubborn, aren't you? *I* see a beautiful, talented young woman who radiates warmth and love. Someone who projects those emotions into her craft and who charmed a very handsome, successful man to the point that he walked into the wrong chapel."

"It was a mistake."

"Maybe it was, but he wouldn't be wanting the mistake to continue if you weren't worth fighting for," Marsali added.

"He just doesn't want to fail. It's a thing with him. He doesn't...he doesn't want to be like his father getting divorce after divorce."

"Izzy, you are a smart, intelligent woman. No man would stay married just to save face," Amelia said.

"He said—"

"We know what he said. And maybe on some small level he meant it," Marsali said, "but men like Everett... Honey, you might not have a large bank account, but he doesn't need that. What Everett needs—what every man *wants*—is someone who balances them. Who has what they don't. They want someone who brings out their protectiveness and adventurous side. Their fun side. I think you do that for him or else he wouldn't still be around."

"That's an awfully big assumption given the fact you've only met him once," Izzy said with a half-hearted smile.

"*Years* of matchmaking experience," Marsali said, the words followed by a wink. "I've learned to size people up very quickly, and the moment Everett walked into your parents' living room, his interest in you was obvious. He could barely take his eyes off of you."

Izzy bit her lip and inhaled, exhaling in a loud rush. "Okay. Okay, so...let's say that's true. That means what? I should go to New York and...and just see what happens? You think it's that easy? What if he *does* want a divorce?"

"You mean what if he gives you the divorce you've asked him for multiple times?" Amelia asked, frowning.

Izzy felt her face flush nine shades of red. "Don't say it. I heard it. I'm royally messed up in the brain."

Amelia chuckled, as did Marsali.

"Think of the trip as a free vacation. No pressure," Marsali added. "Simply enjoy yourself. Have fun exploring the city with a gorgeously handsome man. And don't *ever* doubt what you bring to the table. You're Isabel Shipley, *artiste!* Your paintings are amazing and beautiful and touch people's lives. They'll live on long after we've all grown old and gone. You're painting a legacy, Izzy. One canvas at a time."

"And when the time is right," Amelia said, "you will catch your big break and look back wondering why you ever doubted yourself."

Izzy blinked away the tears stinging her eyes and held out her arms. The two friends moved forward for a group hug. "How did I ever get so lucky to get you as friends?"

"I have a better question," Marsali said. "Amelia, any possibility of getting a hidden camera from the movie set so we can put it on Izzy and go along for the trip?"

"TESSA! YOU GOT A SEC?"

Tessa froze at the sound of the deep voice calling her name, her feet seemingly sticking to the wooden planks of the boardwalk and unable to move. She forced herself to breathe deeply before twisting to see her ex-husband approaching her. Her body went hot and then cold before going hot again because Bruce was a massive man. Tall and broad, even now at sixty-three. He kept in shape, worked out, a fact proven by the muscles straining the width of his shirtsleeves.

Bruce looked handsome as ever in his police uniform. He'd spent his life in uniform. First the military, then the reserves, and now as a long-time policeman who'd spent the last thirty, thirty-five years? Protecting the island.

His dark hair had gone gray shortly after Vietnam, just one of the many tolls battle had taken on an eighteen-year-old kid who'd never been away from home until being sent into the jungle.

"Tess," he said, stopping within breathing distance of her.

His cologne teased her senses and she fought back a smile. After all of these years, he was still an Old Spice man. Some things never changed.

"Bougie has to go for a walk," she blurted, hoping to avoid whatever it was that had her ex speaking to her for the first time since their son had become a teenager and contact between the two adults was no longer necessary.

She'd moved on. Remarried a wonderful if somewhat boring man. He'd been stable, though, and a good father to Jack, and the daughter they'd had next before his passing. She'd stayed widowed a year, working nonstop to keep her business going and raise two small children. Husband number three had been a godsend, her rock through the birth of her third and helping her raise all the children until his recent passing.

"I'll join you. I could use some fresh air," he said, moving next to her and lifting a hand in a gesture to start walking the way she'd been going.

She knew it was ridiculous, but she felt as though every eye was on them, even though her searching glances didn't register anyone she immediately recognized. The boardwalk was as busy as ever, with fisherman unloading trucks and carts to head to the pier. A mom and her young son rode their bikes, his tiny training wheels squeaking with every whirl.

An older woman sat bundled up against the chill in the air, sunglasses on as she read from a thick book while facing the ocean.

The silence between them lengthened, and with every second that passed, she became more nervous as to why the sudden contact. She didn't like it, and warning bells were going off in her brain.

"Tessie, Jack called me," Bruce said finally. "He's worried about his mama."

Her lungs seized and her grip tightened on Bougie's leash. "Why?" Her words were tight, her anger barely suppressed.

"Look, Tessie, I don't want to interfere in your life—"

"Then don't."

"I have to. Because I'm concerned, too."

She stopped walking even though Bougie scented something in the bushes nearby and tugged hard to head in that direction. "You—and Jack—need to respect my boundaries. I don't tell either of you who to date."

"And we're not trying to do that to you. It's just—"

"Just what? *What?*"

For the first time since their awkward conversation began, she felt the full impact of his Bruce's gaze. It sucked the air from her lungs once more, and butterflies danced in her belly.

No. Oh, no. No, no, no! Been there. Done that. Have the divorce papers to prove it!

"Just be careful," Bruce said after a tense moment. "That's all. If what Jack said is true, the guy seems too...smooth."

She knew she should've kept her relationship with Kirk a secret, but Jack had seen the two of them together, and privacy had become a thing of the past at that moment. "Jealous?"

The moment the word slipped from her lips, she ached to take it back. But she couldn't.

Even more astounding was his response. His mouth tightened, his eyebrows pinched over his nose, and for several seconds, a muscle ticked in his jaw.

Wait...was he?

"If you won't protect yourself, at least protect your kids. They might not live at home anymore, but that doesn't mean the men you date have no impact on their lives."

She sucked in a breath to give him a piece of her mind when he turned on his heel, his long strides eating up the distance they'd traveled in no time. She watched as he reached his cruiser and yanked open the door before folding his large frame behind the wheel.

Tessa forced herself to turn away and give Bougie his way, letting the medium-size doodle pull her over to the bushes. She purposely ignored the sound of the cruiser driving toward them on the one-way street, refusing to look up as Bruce slowly drove by.

How dare he? Who did he think he was telling her—*warning her*? Like she was an inexperienced girl. Her anger rose with every passing second. That her son would go behind her back and call his father to... Unbelievable!

Before she knew what was happening, she tugged Bougie along and began marching up the street. The police station wasn't very far away. Only a block. And as angry as she was, she made good time, arriving to find Bruce still sitting in his cruiser, staring down at his computer.

He looked up when her shadow covered the window, his surprise evident before he masked the expression and turned off the ignition. She took a step back and watched as he reluctantly opened the door.

"Before you say anything—"

"Oooh, no," she said with a firm shake of her head. "It's my turn. You? You do not have a say in my life, and if our son ever comes to you again about whomever I might be dating, I demand you tell him it's *none* of your concern and send him to ask me directly."

"Tessie, he's worried."

"There's no reason to be worried."

"You're not acting like yourself," Bruce said.

His gaze moved down her body before returning to her face. "You're even dressing different."

"It's called fashion," she said. "Not to mention the fact that it's winter."

"It's not like you."

Her face burned and she took a step toward him and lifted a hand to poke him in the chest with one finger. "Since when do you care what I wear? Much less what I do...or whom?"

He flinched at her questions, and even though she and Kirk *hadn't* done anything other than make out, it was no one's business but their own.

"I care about you, Tessie. And our son. You know that."

"How would I ever know that?"

The question hung in the air between them, and she saw his confidence falter at the truth of her words.

"I'll always regret how things went down

between us, but you know I've never stopped caring about you."

A low huff of a laugh left her, sarcastic to its core. "Stay out of my business."

"There's something fishy about him."

The hot sting of tears flooded her gaze, and she *hated* the fact that when she got angry, she got teary. "Because he could want me?"

"That's not what I meant at all. Tess—"

"Stop. Go back to avoiding me. Leave me alone."

"I never avoided you."

She glared at him and raised an eyebrow high, noting the slow flush that eventually made his cheeks ruddy. They both knew it was a lie. Because she'd avoided him, too. "Then why are we having this conversion?"

"Jack says the guy is half your age."

So that was the issue? Why was it people considered aging men more attractive but aging women were just...something to be put on the shelf? Not only were women not considered as attractive as their male peers but apparently they were also not as intelligent or as prized despite the very same wrinkles and fat and gray hair that made the men "silver foxes." It was the ultimate smack in the face for women who put their lives on hold to support their husbands' careers. Who put their bodies through horrendous pain in order to carry on the man's name.

And what did most of them have to show for it? "Kirk is younger, yes, but Jack is exaggerating."

"I don't like it. And neither does Jack."

"Well, then it's a good thing I don't care." Having had enough of this conversation despite the fact she'd sought him out the second go-round, she turned and pulled Bougie along with her. Two steps later, Bruce caught her arm in a gentle grip.

"What's his motive, Tessie? Huh? Because my gut is telling me he has one."

She hated that his words made her feel like a fool. An old, ugly, foolish fool. "Maybe he simply likes a woman who knows what she wants. Maybe," she continued "he likes someone mature, who doesn't play the idiotic games so many younger women play."

"You know I don't say this to hurt you."

"Are you sure about that? Because men your age date younger women every single day and people don't seem to have a problem with that."

Bruce had the grace to look embarrassed, but she didn't let it soften her expression. She was so tired of being judged. A woman of her age and standing should do this, shouldn't do that. Why couldn't people mind their own business and live their own lives and forego the gossip and judgment that brought so much pain? "If you'll excuse me, Bougie and I have to get home. Kirk will be there any minute, and after this conversation, I've made a few decisions I can't *wait* to discuss with him."

"Like what?" Bruce growled.

She smiled and reached up to pat his lightly stubbled cheek. "Well, if it was any of your business, maybe I'd tell you."

CHAPTER TWELVE

Late Sunday afternoon, Everett's private jet touched down and Everett escorted Izzy off the plane. He could tell she was a bit wide-eyed at the process of having direct access to the waiting car and the speed with which they were able to get going toward his penthouse. While he'd gotten used to the ability, noting it through her eyes made him remember to be grateful. And thankful for the ability to take what had been an okay business and creating something bigger. "I have a surprise for you when we get home."

She turned her head from the window and met his gaze.

"I think getting me face-to-face time with the gallery curators is plenty enough."

He smiled, glad that a few emails had made her

so happy. "It was my pleasure. I'm happy to have helped, Isabel."

She inhaled and he couldn't help but notice the movement before shifting his gaze back to her face. "I, uh, hope you don't mind but I've taken the liberty of having Jacob make some reservations for us. Places I think you might like to see, tickets to shows, that sort of thing."

Her hand moved to her chest to rub, and he frowned at the gesture. It was one she did often, without thought, and it just dawned on him the cause. "That makes you anxious?"

Her hand stilled its rubbing motion, and she lowered it to her lap once more.

"I *love* surprises," she said, glancing at him, "but I worry that...that you're going to expect things in return that I can't give you."

He shifted on the leather seat and reached out to take her hand in his. "You know my intentions, Isabel. But rest assured I will never pressure you to do anything you don't want to do."

Her fingers were cold, and he lifted them to his lips to warm them before covering her hand with both of his.

"You want to stay married. That's...that's a lot of pressure."

He gazed into her beautiful eyes and wished she could see into his soul. Maybe then it would take her fear away. "I want a chance, it's true."

"Just a chance?"

A slow smile formed on his lips, and he brought her hand up to his mouth once more, this time to rub the softness against the five o'clock shadow on his chin. She felt like silk. "We've done things out of order, that's for certain. But I'd like an honest attempt to connect. For you to get to know me. Ask me questions. Don't just walk away because you think it's what you're supposed to do given our unique start. Can you do that? For me?"

She held his gaze a long moment, the outside world and holiday traffic and all that was the city fading into the background as Tomas took them home.

"I can do that. But just in case it doesn't work, we don't want to postpone things. You'll still have the paperwork drawn up? Ready to sign?"

He didn't like the request, nor the thought of them ending before they'd even had a chance to see where things could go. Izzy was one of a kind. Smart, funny, beautiful. Creative. He loved watching her move, her expressions, her liveliness and energy—after her morning coffee. "Would that take some of the pressure you feel off you? To know you can sign them and leave at any time?"

"It would."

His attorney had drafted something already but hadn't included any form of settlement for Isabel.

That's why he'd told the man to do them again. "Consider it done," he said as a compromise.

"Thank you."

They rode in silence for a while, until Tomas made the turn into the parking garage. Everett squeezed Isabel's hand gently. "I think once we get inside we should change into comfortable clothes and order in. The next few weeks are going to be packed with activities, so a night at home will be a rarity. How does that sound?"

"To an introvert? It sounds perfect."

"I find it hard to see you as an introvert."

She held up the hand he didn't hold and nodded. "I'm an extroverted introvert, which means I love people but only to a point. I can hermit away with some music and canvas and paints and be perfectly satisfied with my own company for very long periods of time."

Tomas parked the car next to the elevator and they exited the vehicle. The ride to the top floor didn't take long, and once the lift doors opened, Everett made a point to watch Isabel's reaction.

"Oh. Wow. Everett, it's beautiful," she breathed, her gaze on the view outside the floor-to-ceiling windows showcasing the city's skyline and the first twinkle of night lights as dusk fell.

She walked toward the windows, and he kept pace with her at her side, smiling at the various expressions crossing her face.

"This is...this is breathtaking."

"Maybe you can paint it while you're here," he murmured.

A frown overtook her features and sadness flickered across her gaze. Smiling inwardly, he grasped her hand and gently tugged. "I'll give you a tour. Come on."

She matched his stride as he showed her the kitchen and dining room, library, his office. "Bedrooms are upstairs. I've had Tomas place your bags in one of the spare rooms down the hall from the master."

He noted the blush taking root in her cheeks and leaned down to whisper, "You're welcome to join me anytime."

She lifted her gaze and shot him an amused glare and he shrugged. "Can't blame a man for trying."

The soft laugh that rumbled out of her compelled him to wrap an arm around her shoulders and squeeze her gently to his side. "Come on. We've got more to see."

"It's not a red room, is it?"

"Ms. Shipley, what have you been watching?" Everett asked in what he hoped was a teasing and seductive tone.

He thought he pulled it off when her face flooded with pretty color.

"All I know is that when someone of your...social

status says there's more, women the world over should be nervous."

"Mmm," he drawled softly near her ear, noting the way she shivered in response. "Don't worry, dear Isabel. I think you'll like the playroom I set up just for you."

IZZY SUCKED in and held her breath when Everett's husky words heated her ear and sent a shock wave of warmth through her. The man could read a phone book and sound sexy.

He led her upstairs, pointing out the different rooms, and then held her gaze while he wrapped a hand around the doorknob of the room at the end of the hall. He started to open it only to hesitate and stare down at her. "What?" she asked, her heart pulsing in her throat. "It's not...it's not a *real* play-room, is it?"

She wasn't sure whether to be horrified...or mournful at never being able to put it to use.

"Brace yourself."

His words left her imagining all sorts of naughty things in the seconds before his hand splayed wide against the black-painted door. It opened silently and she stepped into the room behind him, gaze down until she forced herself to take a look. A laugh

bubbled out of her. Of all the things she'd imagined...
"Seriously?"

Everett's husky chuckle sent another shiver through her as she made a complete circle in the middle of the room, taking in the varying sizes of canvases, a wallboard of paints, containers of brushes and palette knives and positively every single thing she could ever need or want to paint and create. "You had me going there for a second."

He smiled at her.

"If anything's missing, just say the word and I'll have it delivered."

She turned to look at him, her heart cracking open even more despite the danger she tried and failed to warn herself against. Men like Everett wanted well-educated, sophisticated wives, those ready to be the woman behind the man and do whatever it took to help him succeed. Women who led charities and put on fundraisers. She wasn't that kind of woman. And yet...

She didn't remember taking the steps toward him. Didn't remember wrapping her arms around him, but in the next few seconds, she found herself in his arms, face lifted toward his as she tugged his head down for a kiss.

He accepted the invitation and took control immediately, kissing her until her head swam with all the colors of the paint tubes nearby. When he finally lifted his mouth from hers, it took an entire two seconds before she was able to lift her lashes to meet his gaze.

"Remind me to surprise you more often," he murmured, his voice husky. "That was quite the thank you."

It was quite the present. One she couldn't even express her thanks for because, while she'd loved the idea of coming to New York and touring the galleries, she'd hated the fact she'd had to leave her paints and brushes behind. To do this—be so thoughtful and considerate as to provide them here—he'd had to have spent thousands of dollars to set this up.

It was amazing. He was amazing.

His thumb brushed over her lower lip and his gaze followed the movement. She watched him watch his thumb, saw the way his gaze heated. "I c-can't believe you did this."

"I wanted to."

"And I appreciate it. I do, but...it's too much, Everett," she said, taking a step back to break the spell he'd placed on her.

She might have initiated the kiss but he had definitely completed it.

"Consider it an early Christmas present. I thought you might be inspired after your days out and about," he said.

She felt his gaze on her, watching her, as she perused the brushes and paints and ran her fingertips over the many pieces. "It's lovely but it's still too much. I mean, I'll only be here a short time. I can only imagine how much it all cost, and I'd hate to see it wasted. Maybe you should return it?"

"Not a chance."

He closed the distance between them once more, his hands settling over her shoulders gently. He squeezed the tension out of them, thumbs rubbing the tight muscles until she wanted to moan.

"This is for you. Enjoy it, Isabel."

The words whispered into her ear left her swallowing hard and inhaling a shaky breath. "Okay. Thank you. Again. I'll try to put it to good use."

Given the number of canvases in the room, she'd be hard-pressed to use even a few of them before her time in New York came to a close, but she could tell she wasn't going to win this battle. When she left, Everett could do whatever he liked with the remaining items. Maybe a local art school would get a nice donation.

"Stay here and look around, get familiar with everything in case you do see something missing. I'll go order something for dinner. Any requests?"

Requests? How could she ask for more given all he'd already done? "I'd say surprise me but I'm a little afraid to." His rough chuckle drifted over her senses, and she couldn't hold back the smile that formed. "Just don't order the entire menu," she added, lifting a hand to indicate the abundance around them. "Something super simple is fine."

He kissed the top of her head.

"Isabel?"

"Hmm?"

"Welcome home."

MAYBE HE HAD GONE a little overboard, Everett mused later as he sat beside Isabel at the quartz kitchen counter eating dinner. But the joy on her face when she'd seen the room filled to the brim with art supplies had been worth it. He liked that he'd been able to do that for her, give her something that meant so much, even though to him it had only meant a phone call.

"You're staring at me again."

His lips quirked at the corners, and he realized, around Isabel, smiling had become a regular occurrence. "You're beautiful."

She plucked at the pepperoni atop her pizza and plopped it into her mouth. Around it she said, "Flattery will get you nowhere."

"Mmm. Better up my game then."

"Everett—"

"Shh. I meant what I said, Isabel. No pressure," he said with a shake of his head. "But I make no promises to not flirt and tease and do my very best to romance you."

"Divorce isn't failure, you know. Sometimes, it's the best thing to happen even though it's painful and disappointing at the time."

He lifted his hand and brushed a tendril of hair away from her cheek, lingering over the touch because her skin felt so soft. "Are we a bad thing?"

"No. It's just... It's hard to see our weird situation becoming anything more."

Now they were getting somewhere. "Why is that?" he asked, desperate to draw her out and get some insight. With that insight, he could form a battle plan.

Isabel shifted her gaze to his and he watched as she struggled for words. He wanted inside her head. Wanted to know what he was up against when it came to winning the chance to be more. The very fact that she wasn't chomping at the bit to *stay* married now that she knew who he was told him a lot about her. It hinted at her integrity and desire to be true to herself. To do what's right. And maybe if divorcing her didn't meant failure in his mind, he'd be honest enough to say he agreed with the thought. In theory. Under the circumstances, there was no reason to believe they could work. Except...he did believe it.

"I don't see how I can ever fit into your world,"

she said finally. "I'm not schedules and business suits or fancy lunches with the wives of your executives."

He braced his hands on her stool on either side of her hips and leaned toward her, very aware of the way she stiffened in her seat. "I could've found that already, Isabel, if that's what intrigued me."

"S-so it's because I'm a slightly obsessive-compulsive artist that you find me attractive? Sounds to me like you need therapy."

He spread his knees and used his hold to drag her stool the couple of inches separating them, pinning her knees between his and trapping her in his hold. "Maybe," he said softly, "I need a woman unlike myself. Someone to make me remember to appreciate color and life and...a sassy attitude."

"Well, if it's sass you want—"

He kissed her again, gaze on hers until her lashes fluttered low and she hid from him once more. She tasted of pizza and wine, of sass and backtalk and all the things that made Isabel her creative, seductive, fascinating self.

She gasped softly and pulled away, ending the kiss and flicking her tongue over her lower lip in a gesture that made him groan. "Don't do that."

She huffed out a laugh and shook her head. "You're awfully bossy. I don't know if I like a bossy man."

"I beg to differ, Isabel. I remember you liking my bossiness very well."

Color bloomed in her cheeks and he smiled at her response. The primitive part of him loved that he could bring that out in her with a few truthful words. "It's getting late. Would you like to see your room?"

After showing her the makeshift art studio he'd had created for her, they hadn't finished the tour of the penthouse. He'd left her alone to go through her new things like a kid in a candy store, her excitement tangible. He'd ordered them food, and she'd met him in the kitchen a short time later.

"Just tell me where it is. I'm sure I can find it."

He grasped her hand in his and lifted it to his lips to kiss. "Nothing will happen here that you do not wholly consent to, Isabel. I give you my word."

"I-I wouldn't be here if I thought otherwise."

He liked that she trusted him. And he'd do nothing to break that trust. "Good. Now that we have that out of the way, how about we finish the tour?"

CHAPTER THIRTEEN

O n Monday midmorning, her day off from the salon, Tessa inhaled the scent of the roses just delivered to her home and smiled at the note on the card.

Until tonight... Kirk

Some women might consider flowers frivolous, but she loved the thought and effort that went into the gift. She closed the door with her foot and carried the large vase with her into the kitchen, noting the instant upheaval they caused amongst the Babes.

"Well, well, well," Cheryl said.

"What have we here?" Adaline asked.

"Would you look at those," Rayna Jo said.

Only Mary Elizabeth remained silent, and Tessa could feel her friend's worry from across the room.

"So? Who is he?" Cheryl asked.

Tessa set the flowers on the counter and tucked

the card back into the clear plastic holder. "Just a friend."

"A friend who sends *two* dozen roses?" Cheryl *tsked*.

Since Tessa took Sundays and Mondays off, the Babes gathered at her house on Mondays before taking a long walk. Each wore walking shoes and athletic clothes with a stack of jackets and ear warmers piled nearby for the wind coming in off the water. "We're getting to know one another."

Rayna Jo walked over to smell the flowers, her face relaxing as she inhaled.

"I can't remember the last time I got flowers," Rayna Jo said. "They're so beautiful."

"So who is this man?" Cheryl asked.

Tessa gave them a quick rundown of Kirk and how they'd met but left out the part regarding him being younger. Something she noted that Mary Elizabeth picked up on right away if her pursed lips were any indication.

"What does he do?" Cheryl asked.

"He's a businessman. He's working on several large projects right now, including a new restaurant in Carolina Cove."

"Oh, really? Where?" Adaline asked.

"It's just in conception at the moment, I believe. He's looking for investors while trying to firm up details," she said, repeating the news Kirk had told her last night over dinner. He'd surprised her with a call and request to go out and taken her to one of the nicest restaurants in town.

"Is it serious?" Rayna Jo asked.

Tessa felt Mary Elizabeth's stare and shrugged. "I don't know yet. It could get there. Maybe." It was too soon to be thinking about such things, but Kirk had proven himself to be the perfect gentleman. He texted her throughout the day to ask about her well-being, called her at night or took her out. He made a point to come see her, even on his busiest days. That said something about a man, didn't it? That he'd take time out of his day to connect?

"Well, it certainly didn't take long for you to meet someone."

"It just happened," she said in response to Cheryl's statement. "I didn't seek it out. Maybe that's why it's...working so well."

"Just be careful," Mary Elizabeth said.

"When do we get to meet this gentleman?" Rayna Jo asked.

Tessa grabbed her jacket from the pile and shrugged it on, indicating that they needed to get going and hoping it would mean a change in topic. "Soon. I don't know. We'll see."

"It's my turn to host Christmas dinner," Mary Elizabeth said. "Will you be bringing him as your plus-one?"

Tessa glanced at Mary Elizabeth and noted her friend's tense gaze. Why did it matter so much to her? "I don't know yet. Is Izzy bringing her new beau?"

She didn't mean to throw Izzy under the bus, so to speak, but she felt Mary Elizabeth needed the reminder that there were other people she needed to concern herself with more, namely her youngest daughter.

Tessa had enough life experience under her belt to weather whatever storms appeared, and Mary Elizabeth should know that. So should her children and her ex, she thought, anger spiking despite her attempts to stay calm. "Ladies, time to head out. Shall we?"

The other Babes apparently sensed the tension in the room if the exchange of glances Tessa witnessed was any indication. They moved to don jackets and gloves for the windy walk, and Tessa waited impatiently for them to finish before opening her door.

"I'm just worried about you, you know," Mary Elizabeth murmured as she moved by Tessa out the door.

"Don't be. Kirk and I are fine. You'll see." The words sounded terse and argumentative, but Tessa couldn't help it. She was too old to be dealing with this type of nosiness, even from her best friends. "As to Christmas dinner, I'll ask Kirk to join us. How about that?"

THE NEXT FEW days flew by in a whirlwind of activity for Izzy. She couldn't have asked for a better or more gentlemanly host in Everett. Every day he and Jacob closed themselves in Everett's office for several hours to work, and Izzy used the time to organize her temporary studio. By day two, she had things as she liked them and prepped her canvas to begin something new.

Having done mostly seascapes, she remembered Everett's words about cityscapes. She chose her palette of colors and set her easel up in front of the windows. Outside, the sky was overcast and a light drizzle pelted down from above. She gazed down at the traffic below, and in an instant, her mind flashed with the image she wanted to paint.

She lost herself in the process, the sound of her brush swirling over the canvas as she created the moody gray sky, the rain-dampened buildings and blur of lights on glass. She pictured a woman on the street, black dress and flowy raincoat, a Victorian-era umbrella covering her upper body as she hustled to get out of the weather.

Izzy lifted her brush and took a step back, staring at the picture that had poured out of her in precise detail. Only one thing was missing. Biting her lip, she dipped her brush into the black again and outlined an image. Male. Broad shoulders dressed in a suit, dark head bare as he walked several steps behind the woman, his stride long as though he tried to catch up to her.

In an instant she knew the title of her work. *The Pursuit.*

Her breath turned shallow as she added the fine lines and details required. The shine and shadow of his rain-logged Italian leather loafers, the thickness of his hands. The purposeful intensity of his body.

She stopped once more and took another step back, tilted her head to the side as she looked for things to fix or adjust. There were none. At least at the moment.

Izzy glanced at her watch and noted the time. The painting had taken shape so quickly she had time to start another if she wanted. Everett wouldn't be ready to go out for their afternoon adventure for at least another hour.

Izzy moved the first painting to the wall to dry and set about prepping another canvas. She'd take a look at her first work tomorrow. See if it needed more after some time away from it.

Canvas prepped, she followed a drop of rain as it trickled down the window across from her.

This time the image that appeared was one of the woman alone. She was in a park, sitting on a bench, watching a fountain spew water up in the air. Her face was only partially visible, more shadows and hollows than distinct features. She held a book on her lap, pen in hand, but her gaze was on the fountain.

Daydreaming.

Getting away from Carolina Cove and coming to New York with Everett had definitely stirred her creativity. Images and titles burst out of her, faster than she could paint them. Yet another gift from Everett, even though this one was born from within her rather than given.

These images were a little darker due to the gray of the concrete around her subjects, but no less compelling in the mood they evoked. She lost herself in the joy of her art and jumped when strong hands lightly landed on her shoulders. "Oh!"

Everett's low chuckle caressed her in a touch.

"I'm sorry. I didn't mean to scare you. I called your name twice but you were very into it."

She turned to face him and watched as his smile widened before he reached up and gently wiped his thumb over her cheek.

"You're your own work of art," he murmured, holding up the thumb for her to see.

Izzy shrugged and smiled. "Occupational hazard," she quipped. "I never know where I'll find paint."

The moment the words left her mouth, she realized the imagery they portrayed. Heat fused her cheeks once more, and she wondered if she'd ever get to a point where she wasn't tongue-tied around Everett.

"Hmm. Maybe I should check you over. To help," he suggested with a wicked grin.

She forced herself to narrow her gaze and hold up the brush in warning. "Don't even think about it. You said no sex."

"Did I?"

"Yes. And...I'm holding you to it."

"Shame. I suddenly have an urge to buy body paint. Are you sure you're not interested?"

The man could turn a nun into a pole dancer with his words and the look in his eyes. "What, um, are we doing today?"

"Do you think changing the subject will help?"

"Can't hurt."

He grinned again and she shot him a wary look as she set about cleaning her brushes.

"You have a meeting with one of the gallery cura-tors this afternoon in"—he checked his watch—"about two hours."

"Two hours? Are you... *Two hours?*" She looked at the mess she'd made of paints and gesso and brushes and cleaner. "Why didn't you tell me before now?"

"I didn't want you to get nervous."

"Yeah, well, guess what? It didn't work!" She scrambled to organize the mess she'd made, well aware of Everett watching her every move.

By the time she got everything cleaned and put away, she'd lost a solid twenty minutes. "I have to go shower. What am I going to wear? If you'd told me, I could've had this figured out already!"

"Isabel."

She stopped her hasty exit and turned to see him still standing right where he'd been all along. "What?"

He moved toward her, every step slow and deliberate, like an animal stalking its prey but without the threat of death, she mused. Well, if one didn't count the fact she wanted to kill him.

Everett cupped her face in his palms and lowered his head toward hers. Her breath turned shallow and she parted her lips in welcome. Kissing Everett was never a chore or a bother. That much she knew for certain. It was the only thing she knew for certain.

After a slow, sweet, mind-whirling kiss, he lifted his lips from hers and brushed them against her forehead.

"Breathe. You've got this, sweetheart. They'll be putty in your hands."

Izzy closed her eyes and embraced the moment. The gesture.

Could anything be as romantic and wonderful as Everett stating that he believed in her?

ISABEL INSISTED SHE GO ALONE. She understood that Everett had gotten her foot in the door, but
now? It was up to her to make the connection work
for her. If she couldn't do that, then she had no business playing with the big dogs.

"Beautiful," Max, the curator, said. "I'll admit it's
not our normal style of showcase but you have a defi-
nite talent, Ms. Shipley."

"Isabel, please. Or Izzy," she said before ordering
herself to stop before she came across like an idiot.

"You convey emotions very well. Not only with
color but the lines. Your work has feeling and
movement."

Pride burst throughout her body, and she felt her
face flush with pleasure. "Thank you. That's high
praise coming from you."

Max set his iPad aside and leaned back in his
office chair. "Are you working on anything now?"

"Actually, yes," she said, silently thanking Everett
yet again for the makeshift studio in his penthouse. It
was the gift that kept giving. "I've completed two
pieces since arriving in town."

"Impressive. You haven't been here long, have
you?"

"No, but...the city inspires me." It was true. Her
heart would always belong to the beach she loved so
much, but right now she loved the change of scenery.
The difference in lighting and textures, the pace of
the city over the more relaxed feel of island time. "I'm

loving the contrast between the concrete and block buildings and the people passing by. To me there seems to be many ways of looking at them. Whether the people are happy or sad, or the buildings reflect their purpose. It's a different energy than my seascapes."

"Intriguing. Have you given any thought to having a show here? I do believe my colleagues would approve sponsoring such an event."

Heart in her throat, she clenched her fingers together until the pain forced her to focus. "I...am certainly open to the option."

"That's good to hear," Max said. "As to what I have in mind..."

THE MOMENT ISABEL stepped from the building, Everett knew her meeting had been a success. She hadn't seen him yet, standing across the street waiting for her exit, but she carried her head high, every line of her beautiful body graceful as she moved toward the curb.

She spotted him then, and as their gazes locked, Everett felt his heart squeeze a bit. She looked happy, and happy on Isabel was a sight to behold. He liked the thought that he'd had some small influence in that.

A horn blared at her, and Tomas and Everett

both stepped forward when Isabel almost stepped into the street against the traffic light. She jumped back at the last second and his gut tightened at the near disaster. Across the street, he watched as she bit her lip and lifted her shoulders in a shrug, drawing a laugh from him despite the danger she'd been in.

He shook his head at her antics and, once the light changed, met her halfway across the street to take her arm and escort her to the car.

"Okay, so I might be a little excited," she said, practically dancing at his side. "But that meeting? Everett, how can I ever thank you?"

He could think of a few ways. But he kept those thoughts to himself. For now. "Tell me everything over dinner."

A laugh bubbled out of her, the sound light and airy and fun. It lifted his mood even more.

Everett helped her into the car and told Tomas to take them to Everett's favorite restaurant. He'd had Jacob make a reservation even though it hadn't been needed. He could go anywhere in the city and get a table, but he hadn't wanted to risk an unwanted delay. Tonight was about celebrating her success and planning the next step. "So?"

"Ah! He wants to do a showcase! I can't believe it. Of course, I kept it cool in there, but oh, my word, a showcase!"

Everett chuckled at her excitement. "Congratulations. I knew you could do it."

Her smile fell just a bit before turning into a frown.

"Everett, you didn't have anything to do with this, did you? I mean, you didn't, like, convince him to offer it as a favor or something, right?"

He supposed every artist felt insecure about their work, but it broke his heart that Isabel was one of them. Had no one ever believed in her? "No, sweetheart. All I did was send the pictures. You and your talent did the rest. I promise."

His words must have reassured her because the smile returned and warmed his heart.

"It's so surreal."

"Well, you'd best get used to it. Don't forget you have at least one more meeting to go to."

She shook her head and stared across the seat at him, eyes glittering with the sheen of tears.

"Thank you."

He grasped her hand in his and lifted it to his lips, brushing her knuckles with a kiss. "You're welcome."

She stared at him a long moment before leaning over and pressing her lips to his in a quick kiss.

He kept his eyes on hers, watching her, needing to hold on to the image. "If I get free kisses every time I help you..."

The words emerged as a growl but it couldn't be helped. He wanted her—his wife. More and more every passing day.

A blush rose into her cheeks and he grinned at the result. His sweet Isabel. "Dinner then dancing," he said, whispering the words into her hair. One good thing that had come from that horrible private school was dance lessons.

"Dancing?"

He nodded. She wasn't ready for more between them, but maybe until then, he could dance his way into her heart?

CHAPTER FOURTEEN

T he following evening, Isabel set her brush
aside and stepped back, lifting her arms
over her shoulders to stretch high on her
tiptoes. She'd been at it since she'd woken up this
morning and now had a third picture to send to
Maxwell Lucas in regard to her potential showcase.
Getting the offer was one thing, but as Everett had
advised over dinner, she shouldn't accept until
meeting with the other curator to see what they had
to offer as well.

And today her work had taken a bit of a turn, but
she liked it. A lot.

On the way into the restaurant last night, her
gaze had been captured by the brick entrance. Old-
school. Black awning. Black door. Sort of mysterious.
The interior had made her think of speakeasies from
the 1920s. That led to fashion, and her painting

today had taken shape within moments of putting brush to canvas.

A long, feminine leg, short black fringe, hairpiece made of feathers and sparkles, red lipstick. The woman sat on a stool at a bar, head down, lips pouted, as she stared deeply into her drink. *Reflection*, her mind whispered. And she knew the title fit well. Who hadn't had that moment of reflection while pondering life's choices?

She'd already planned a series around the speakeasy vibe, knowing she could play upon the seductiveness of the time period, the awareness of the emotions Maxwell Lucas had found so intriguing.

Emotions came in all forms. Weather, dress, facial features, lighting. Even hair. Soft, flowing hair or tight knot?

She grabbed another canvas she'd already prepped and started on it, losing herself in the mechanics of creating. In the art of shadows and light.

Isabel.

"Isabel?"

Large hands descended on her shoulders, and she squeaked out a frightened gasp. Everett. "You scared me again."

"Sorry. It's late. You need to rest."

"I'm working. I'm good."

"Isabel, tomorrow night is the gala. I don't want

you falling asleep on me."

The gala. One of the events she'd promised Everett she'd attend.

"The stylist will be here in a few hours, too."

She turned to face him and sucked in a sharp breath. Everett stood shirtless, gray sweatpants slung low on his hips. "What time is it?"

"Three thirty. You've been at this all day. I know artists create while the iron is hot but you need to rest."

"My meeting with the gallery is the day after tomorrow—er, today."

"I'm well aware. But it'll do you no good to sleep through it, either."

His gently calloused hands framed her face and lifted it so she had to meet his gaze. She didn't mind. It kept her eyes off his chest and the muscles there. This was an Everett she hadn't painted. One that needed to be. *Soon.*

"Cover your paints. You're going to bed."

"You can't—"

"I can. I need you at my side at your best, Isabel. Not worn out and exhausted. Cover your paints while you have the chance or they won't get covered."

Sensing he meant it, she huffed as she turned and draped a cloth over her paints, determined to fix things properly after a couple hours' sleep.

"Good. Bed for you."

"I can take myself to bed, Everett."

He chuckled and moved toward her in such a way she took a step back, another, all the way to the door of the makeshift studio until he locked it before pulling it closed behind them.

"Hey!"

"Bed," he ordered, looking far too serious and...gorgeous.

"Fine. But only because of the gala. Then it's right back to it."

"Whatever you say, sweetheart."

He took her hand in his and led her down the hallway to her bedroom. She glanced at his open bedroom door along the way.

"Isabel?"

"What?" She shifted her gaze to his and found him watching her.

"What are you thinking, wife?"

The air left her lungs in a rush as his huskily murmured words drifted over her. They'd reached her door by then, but only a few more steps would take her back to his. "Nothing. I-I'm tired."

His gaze glittered as he stared down at her. Amusement? Patience?

He drew her close and pressed his lips to hers.

"My door is always open to you, sweetheart. Good night, Isabel."

She fumbled to turn the knob of her door and practically fell inside before shutting it behind her and pressing her back against the panel.

Seductive Everett was a force to be reckoned with—and one she had to sketch. *Now.* Before the image faded away like the way their marriage would end.

"YOU KNOW EVERETT DRAKE?" Kirk said with a shake of his head in Tessa's direction.

They'd gone to dinner and then for a walk along the beach and now sat on her couch having a nightcap. "Not really. I only met him recently but Isabel seems quite taken with him."

"I'd say. Man, what I wouldn't give to be able to bend his ear for a while. That man knows more about business than anyone."

"Really? He seems too young for that." Tessa took a sip of her wine and listened as Kirk expounded on Everett's business acumen. It took a while. But when he finished, she smiled at him. "If he returns with Isabel, perhaps I could arrange a meeting between you. No promises," she said quickly. "But the girls are already planning a New Year's Eve celebration. Mary Elizabeth assumes Everett will join Isabel, but no one is certain."

"Tessa, sweetheart, that would be great. Thank you. Wow. It's just... I have things rolling for this project I'm working on, but one of my investors just reneged and pulled out. I'd love to know what

Everett would do in that situation. I mean, I had people lined up before, but they've moved on to other things. Now I'm scrambling to keep all the balls in the air."

"That's understandable." Owning her own business, she knew well the problems too little cash flow could cause.

"At least it wasn't one of the big guns. I mean, I should be able to find someone to fund fifty grand, no problem, right? It's not *that* much. I'd do it myself but I'm already all in and skating by." He broke off and shook his head. "I'm sorry. No woman wants to hear that from her man."

Her man? Was that really how he saw himself? The thought made her smile. "No, it's fine. Although I wouldn't have let you take me to such a luxurious dinner again had I known." He'd taken her to one of the upscale restaurants in Wrightsville Beach, one where a bottle of wine cost a week's worth of groceries.

"I wanted to."

"You spoil me."

"You deserve to be spoiled. Tess—"

Kirk broke off and she wondered at his words. "What?" she asked, feeling like a schoolgirl with the way he looked at her.

"You're just...you're beautiful. Amazing. I'm having so much fun with you. I hope you feel the same?"

He leaned forward and lifted his hand to caress her face, letting his fingertips glide over her smooth skin. Thank God she owned a salon, which forced her to keep up her appearance, because otherwise her old woman chin would've been apparent. "I'm having fun with you, too."

"Yeah?"

She sucked in a breath when she watched his head lower toward hers. He'd kissed her before. Many, many times. Light brushes over her lips or cheeks. But this...the look in his eyes...

Her lungs seized as his mouth settled over hers. Kirk pressed and she allowed the embrace to deepen. By the time he lifted his head, her heart raced and she wondered if she'd dreamed it. He'd seemed so passionate, like he didn't notice her wrinkles and lines and the years of difference she couldn't hide if she tried. And, oh, she tried.

"You're blushing," he said, amusement in his tone.

"Are you surprised a woman of my age and experience can still blush?"

"Hush. You're gorgeous and you know it."

His words sank deep and she hated that they meant so much to her. "You know, I have some fun money set aside. Maybe...maybe I could be your investor. To replace the one that withdrew?"

He leaned back and immediately shook his head. "No. No, I can't ask you to do that."

"You're not asking. I'm offering." She'd been

saving up for years to take one of those spa months where you get nips and tucks and facials along with a luxurious recovery period where you came home looking like a new woman—literally. But when Kirk looked at her the way he did, just as she was, helping him seemed more important.

"Tessa...I can't accept. It's too much."

"You can accept. I insist," she said with a heartfelt smile. "I like the thought of helping build my community. Just give me the paperwork and I'll make out a check and sign."

Kirk gaped at her, looking relieved and grateful and seductive all at once.

"You're unbelievable. Come here."

He pulled her to him and lowered his head, kissed her again and again and again...

EVERETT LIFTED his head at the sound of a footfall on the stairs and sucked in a deep breath at the sight of Isabel in her gala dress. He'd known she'd look beautiful. She always did, whether made up for the day or makeup free with her hair in a messy bun and paint-stained clothes. But this woman... "Wow."

A slow smile formed on her lips and he bit back a groan. He wanted to kiss those lips but doing so would muss her makeup. And while that wasn't a bad idea in the slightest, they had to go, and he knew if he started kissing her, he wouldn't want to stop.

"So do I pass inspection?" she asked once she'd made it to the bottom of the stairs.

He set his drink aside and moved toward her, taking her hand in his and lifting it to his lips. She wore a strapless Christmas red lace gown that hugged every curve of her body, with an added solid layer of material at her waist that formed a longer skirt and bit of a train. The dress was dramatic and artistic and absolutely perfect for her. "You make me want to stay here, Isabel."

She flushed in response to his words, and he lightly licked her knuckle to get her taste before kissing it. "Let me," he said, releasing her hand to take her coat.

She turned and he placed it around her shoulders. "This dress makes me want to take you shopping just so I can see more of these on you."

She turned her head and gazed at him over her shoulder. "Careful. You're sounding a little possessive there, Drake."

He gently squeezed her shoulders and turned her to face him once more. "When it comes to you, I'm discovering that I am."

She blinked up at him, gorgeous lips parted.

"Everett..."

"Isabel." He smiled at her expression, identifying her conflicted emotions as they crossed her features.

"Don't worry about my possessiveness right now. Let's go get this over with."

Isabel remained silent as Tomas drove them to their destination. He watched her profile as she stared out the window at the window displays and people, very well aware of the moment she turned her head slightly to sneak a peek at him from beneath her long lashes.

Finally she cleared her throat.

"You, um, look very handsome in your tuxedo."

He stretched out his arm and gently tugged her to his side, using his other hand to tilt her head up. "One day soon, Isabel, we are going to have a very detailed chat."

She swallowed and he felt the movement of her muscles against the back of his fingers curled against her throat.

"About what?"

"You know what," he murmured.

She closed her eyes for a long moment before blinking them open and holding his gaze.

"You really think we could make this work?"

He brushed his lips against her forehead and held her close. "I do."

They arrived moments later and a valet opened their door. Everett exited first and extended his hand to Isabel. She swiveled her long legs out, the split in her dress giving him and the valet a glimpse of pale flesh and sparkling high heels as she stood.

His grip tightened on her hand and he tucked her to his side. "I like that dress," he growled into her ear.

She giggled, and in that moment, Everett knew he was a total goner. Somehow, someway, he had to convince her. That or lock her up and throw away the key.

"Mr. Drake, this way!"

"Mr. Drake, over here!"

"Mr. Drake, who is your lovely companion tonight?"

"Is it serious, Mr. Drake?"

Everett felt Isabel's desire to turn and run into the building to escape the flashing lights of the media outside the highly publicized event, but he tucked her to his side and held tight, giving them the pictures they wanted. "Smile," he murmured into her ear.

The flashes intensified as Isabel did, and Everett had a good idea of what they looked like with his murmuring into her ear, smiling, while she responded. And even though some might think it was all part of a game, it wasn't. Somewhere along the way, his feelings for his newfound wife had solidified into something more. Something he couldn't allow himself to acknowledge considering she still thought of walking away.

HOURS LATER ISABEL LEFT THE LADIES' room and spotted the exit to the rooftop garden. The twinkling lights drew her, and she pressed through the doorway, breathing in the crisp air. The party was everything extravagant and delectable, but the crush of people and noise had started to give her a headache. Her feet ached in the heels, more proof she'd spent far too much time barefoot at the beach, if such a thing existed.

Could anyone ever spend too much time with their toes in the sand?

The question prompted more, and she wandered through the maze of potted plants and shrubs, unable to come up with an answer. Everett obviously thrived in the city, and to be fair, she had as well since being here.

The city had opened up her creativity, introducing her to new sights and textures, and she loved the results slowly appearing on her canvases. Just thinking about her art made her want to find an exit and leave the party to go play in her paints because that's where she felt most at home.

Carolina Cove. New York City. Everett. Their alone time together had strengthened her feelings for him. She'd be lying if she said otherwise. But the rational part of her brain still floundered when it came to the speed of their relationship and the heartbreak at risk.

Insta-love only happened in romance novels and

ninety-minute rom-coms. Not real life. No Las Vegas stranger turned out to be husband material, much less billionaire husband material.

"You left me defenseless in there," Everett murmured.

She turned to find him watching her, hands tucked into his tuxedo pants like the rich, gorgeous businessman he was.

That was yet another thing to ponder. She'd grown up in a wealthy family, even though she'd been on her own for a while now. Still, Everett was on a whole other level of wealth she couldn't even fathom.

"What's got your mind going in circles, sweetheart? Did someone say something to you?"

He seemed genuinely concerned and upset on her behalf of some slight, and she shook her head. "No."

Everett stepped closer, and she waited for the zing of electricity to fill her body when his hands landed on her upper arms.

"You're chilled."

"It was too hot inside. I needed some air."

"What's going on, Isabel?"

She stared up at him, deciding it was time to get real, even though it meant saying some things he probably didn't want to hear. "Why are you so insistent on making this work? Is it...is it *because* there's no prenup? Are you afraid I'm going to demand money from you? Because I won't. It was an honest mistake and I don't want anything from you. You've already done more than anyone sho—"

He lowered his head and kissed her, silenced her. Not a light, brief kiss but one that stole her breath and trapped her soul. A kiss that destroyed her lipstick and left her clinging to him for support just to stay upright.

By the time Everett lifted his mouth from hers, they were both breathing heavily. Without a word, he snagged her hand in his and led her through the maze to the door and then the elevator. Thankfully it was unoccupied as the party was still in full swing. Everett didn't say anything as he pulled her onto the elevator with him, but the moment the doors closed, he pressed her against the wall and kissed her again.

By the time the elevator doors opened, Isabel's mind swirled with hazy what-ifs, and she watched with dazed eyes while he stooped to pick up the clutch she hadn't even known she'd dropped.

The coat check saw them coming and scrambled to retrieve their outerwear. Isabel hurried to keep up with Everett's long strides, aching feet nearly forgotten in the magical bliss he'd created with his kisses.

The moment they were in the car, Everett rolled up the tinted privacy screen and pulled her across the seat onto his lap. She didn't protest, even though she knew she should.

One kiss led to three and those led to more. She trembled uncontrollably by the time they made it to the parking garage, and when she stumbled on the way to the lift, Everett bent and swooped her up into his arms.

He held her on the elevator, carried her through the penthouse, up the stairs. In the hallway between her bedroom door and his, he slowly lowered her to her feet.

She struggled to breathe properly, knowing that this was truly her moment of choice. Everett's gaze locked on hers, hot and intense, his silent question obvious. Did she go to her room and shut the door in his face and on all the progress they'd made? Or take his hand and lead him to the master, taking yet another step toward the life Everett said he wanted?

Izzy swallowed hard and took several moments to breathe as the potential and the ramifications raced through her mind like a hurricane. It wasn't until she felt the sharp poke of the doorknob against her hip that she realized her body had moved of its own accord.

Holding his gaze, she found the doorknob with her hand and twisted. The moment she stepped over the threshold into his room, Everett pounced, dragging her up against him with his hands beneath her hips, lifting her so that her face was level with his.

"Mine," he muttered against her lips.

CHAPTER FIFTEEN

The following evening, Everett watched as Isabel struggled to stay upright on the ice skates, a smile hovering on his lips as he held her hands and countered her fumbles to keep them both on their feet.

"There's a reason I'm a beach girl," she growled. "Remind me to take you surfing and let's see how well you do."

He laughed, loving her competitive streak. "You haven't fallen for about three minutes."

The glare she shot him from beneath her lashes left him chuckling, and with a curl of his arm, he brought her round so that she pressed against his front. "Kiss me."

Without protest, she used his chest for balance and heeded his request, and he kept them both upright even when her feet slipped on the ice in opposite directions. "Had enough skating?"

"Have mercy, *yes.*"

Another laugh ripped out of him, and he gripped her tight, slowly managing to get her to the outside wall with only a few wobbles and one last-minute catch to keep her from falling on her pretty rear.

The skates came off, and once they were back in street shoes, he wrapped his arm around her and left the area to peruse the famous shop windows, Tomas falling into step behind them as their ever-present guard.

Everett loved exploring the city through Isabel's eyes. She truly had an artist's soul in that he'd often catch her looking at people or structures or things of interest, a tilt to her head as she studied them.

He liked her quiet contemplation, but not nearly as much as he liked her laughing and seductive and looking sleep-tousled and gorgeous wearing one of his dress shirts. Those were images he'd carry in his heart and mind forever.

After another hour of strolling the streets of New York and taking in all the Christmas lights and sounds, they headed back to the penthouse. It had taken massive amounts of persuasion to lure Isabel out of her studio this afternoon, and while he loved her passion for her work—something he totally understood and supported—he wanted to spend every moment he could with her.

"Tired?" he asked once they'd shed their coats and gloves and hats.

As though sensing his mood, she bit her lower lip and shook her head. "No, but I should probably get back to work. The meeting with the curator is coming up, and I want to have new art to show her."

"Can I see what you've been working on?"

She worried her lower lip between her teeth, but after a few seconds, she nodded. "If you'd like."

He followed her to the bedroom turned studio, noting the sway of her hips and the way her hat had mussed her hair. The tip of her nose was red from the cold, and her mascara was smudged from her wind-induced tears.

He liked that she didn't look perfect. This Isabel was soft and gentle, creative and fun. A woman who didn't know her own allure and made him thankful of it.

She flipped the light switch in the room, and he paused in the doorway. Her large easel held a painting draped with fabric, but around the room were several projects she'd completed, setting atop smaller tabletop easels or blanketed tables to dry.

He moved through the room, pausing at the first piece, amazed at her speed and skill. He immediately knew where she'd gotten her inspiration and liked the fact him showing her the city had helped inspire her. The woman Isabel had painted looked lonely yet strong, sad but not broken, staring into the depths of her drink as though remembering a heartbreak or some other important moment in her life.

From there he moved on to the second piece, liking the vibe and continuity of the set. This image was of the same woman, walking alone in a rain-soaked street.

The third canvas... His face was in shadow and not visibly defined. The image was more about his physique, but it was obviously him, right down to the gray sweatpants and watch on his arm. He was the focus of the painting, but in the background was a feminine shape and hair the color of Isabel's. "Have you titled it?"

He heard her swallow audibly.

"The...The Waiting Game."

He smiled inwardly and nodded before moving on, pausing to finger the drape hanging on the wood of the easel yet not over the work itself. "May I?" he asked, respectful of her wishes to wait until a piece was finished. Maybe she'd forgotten to cover it, thinking no one would be in here but her.

"Oh, it...it was just a quick one. I did it today before we... I...guess."

He immediately stepped in front of the easel before she could change her mind and shifted his gaze from her to the image.

He exhaled in a *whoosh,* his lungs seizing at the sight of a couple, the man standing tall and bare-chested behind a smaller woman, arms cradling her while she wore his dress shirt. His head was buried in her neck, her head tilted at an angle to give easy access, lips parted as she breathed. The watch was there. Isabel's hair hid the majority of her face as she pressed it against the arm securing her. "This one is sold."

"What?"

"I want it. Name your price."

"Everett, it's not really... I thought maybe I'd—"

"I want it," he said, turning his head to meet her gaze. "Does it have a name?"

A blush surged into her cheeks, confirming his thoughts as to the models.

"The M-morning After."

Once again he nodded. She had a gift for naming her works. One that carried with it the very emotions painted for the world to see. This moment of tenderness and warmth, seduction and desire. Their morning after—not the one in Vegas when she'd disappeared.

"You can h-have it," Isabel murmured. "If you'd like. Consider it a Christmas gift. It's not like I'd know what to get you otherwise."

He left the painting and closed the distance between them, tugging her gently into his arms and then framing her face with his hands. "It's all I want —and you."

The air stilled and became charged with electricity. They both knew her time in New York was coming to an end unless she chose to stay. Unless he did something, said something, to convince her to take the chance fate had given them by crossing the threshold of that chapel door.

Everett lowered his head, kissed her with every ounce of the pent-up frustration he felt that the days were passing so quickly. Then he lifted her up and carried her to the nearby sofa.

ISABEL FOUGHT the urge to hurl due to nerves and followed the young restaurant host to the table where the gallery curator waited.

"Ms. Shipley," the woman said, smiling.

Isabel held out her hand in greeting. "Isabel, please."

"And you can call me Margo," the older woman said, waving a hand at the chair opposite her. Isabel took a moment to remove her coat and set it in the seat beside her before settling in herself. "Thank you for meeting with me."

"It's my pleasure. When I saw your work, I knew we'd be a good fit. Your paintings have the relaxed feel and sensuality we're going for right now. That's a huge draw for me."

"Thank you."

"I mean it. Your work has a modern look, yet a *vibrancy*," the woman exclaimed. "It's like stepping into a book or a movie scene. You capture the moments and make them come to life."

The words left her speechless. "I-I don't know what to say. Thank you. That's quite the compliment."

"I wouldn't say it if it wasn't true," Margo said.

"May I get your drink order?"

Isabel looked up at the waitress and smiled. "Just coffee for me, thanks."

"No cocktail?" Margo asked Isabel. "I'd hoped we'd be celebrating."

Isabel laughed and shook her head. "It's best I keep a clear head."

"I understand. No doubt you'll leave here and get back to work."

"Yes. That's the plan."

"Well, don't discount refilling the creative well. There's lots to do in this beautiful city. I hope you're exploring it."

"I am. Trust me." Isabel looked up and accepted the coffee from the fast-moving waitress. After doctoring it with sugar and cream, she lifted it for a long sip.

"Before I start, do you happen to have any other work to show me?"

"Oh, yes." Izzy pulled out her iPad and swiped a finger over the screen. She'd taken careful photos of her latest work this morning and hoped they were as impactful on the gallery curator as they seemingly had been on Everett.

While Margo studied the images, Izzy's thoughts returned to the man at the penthouse waiting for her call.

They'd shared yet another wonderful night together, and she knew she was losing her resolve when it came to Everett. It was becoming harder and harder to remember all the reasons why they shouldn't be together. Especially when he was the complete package.

Handsome, intelligent, kind. He could seem a bit stuffy at times, but she'd learned the art of teasing him out of that, reveling in her ability to make him smile. Everett was tender and nurturing, bringing her coffee and tea and even snacks, during the day when he took a break from his heavy workload to come check on her in the studio.

"Oh, my dear..." Margo said.

Isabel glanced at the image, knowing in her heart of hearts which one it was. She'd poured herself into that piece, even though it had taken shape faster than any other she'd painted. "I'm afraid that piece is already sold."

"So I see," Margo said, finger tapping on the red tag Isabel had pasted over the corner to keep things simple. "Is it still available for showing?"

"Oh, um...perhaps? I can ask the buyer if th-they

would be willing to delay acceptance. If we do a show, I mean."

"Please do. And as to a show—yes, my dear, I'd be honored to sponsor one for you. I so hope you'll say yes." Margo flipped back to the beginning of Izzy's portfolio and started over again. "But first let me explain. We've started something new in order to draw in a younger crowd. It's different than most normal gallery shows, but I think you might like it."

Izzy watched as the woman took in her attire, her gaze sweeping over her clothes to her necklace, earrings, and even the bracelets on her arm. The clothes were Amelia's, but they'd paired well with the costume jewelry Izzy had picked up over the years.

Margo went on to explain how her physical gallery had closed due to Covid and wasn't a true brick-and-mortar structure any longer. That said, it was still in business and moved throughout the city whenever they found an artist they felt strongly about featuring.

"Oh, but I don't have a following. At least not much of one. My customers are all mostly in the Carolinas."

"Yes, but we can work with that. Your beach-scapes could represent anywhere in the world, and these"—she waved a hand over the iPad—"are time-less." Margo continued, "We keep the guest list tight, *exclusive*, and directions to the showcase aren't even made public until the last possible moment, adding to the mystique of the artist who will be featured."

"Oh, how fun," Isabel said, having never heard of such a thing.

"Right? It's something new we're trying. We've only done one other showcase like this as a trial run, but our clients ate it up, and it was one of our most successful shows *ever*."

"So would I share the showcase with other artists?" She wondered if she had enough work to fill something of that scale.

"No. It's only one artist per showcase so the focus is on you—and items you personally curate as contributing art."

Contributing art? "I don't understand." Items *she* would curate?

"Your art is the focus, of course, but we want it showcased in a home setting. So buyers can see how it would look in their own home. Things like nice throws or pillows, small pieces of furniture like settees, ottomans. Perhaps costume jewelry like you're wearing, or clothing close in feel to what your art displays? Complimentary decor that highlights your art in every way and makes the buyers want the complete package."

"Window dressing."

"Yes, exactly."

She could see it. Like staging a house for resale,

her art would be enhanced by the items she chose to go with it.

Her imagination went wild with ideas. Her beach images were easy. Wraps and gauzy coverups, big, floppy hats, along with hammered rings and bracelets, anklets. Driftwood tables, seagrass baskets. Oversized seashells? Designer towels? She could see where the Hamptons crowd would definitely enjoy having the matching done for them and the artwork to boot.

As to her latest pieces, maybe she could showcase a watch like Everett wore? Would a jewelry store loan such a thing if they thought they might sell it? Didn't Hollywood celebs "borrow" jewelry all the time for events? But what about the rest? She couldn't exactly cover the cost of the items, especially when they weren't guaranteed to sell, and she couldn't ask Everett after everything he'd already done for her. It was too much.

"I can see your mind whirling with ideas," Margo said, a wide smile on her face. "Does this mean you accept? You'll be one of our showcases? We've been narrowing down candidates for our next one, but I knew the moment Mr. Drake sent that email that I just had to have you. Say yes, Isabel."

ISABEL DIDN'T GO HOME after her meeting. She'd left Margo with a promise to get in touch once she finalized her answer, but the last thing she wanted was to promise something she couldn't deliver. And when it came to "curating" the other items that would go with her show, she wasn't sure how to go about it.

The gallery would give her a small stipend, which would be reimbursed before she was paid— unless, of course, she wanted to front the expense of the curated items entirely. Then, the gallery would simply take a percentage of her sales after marking things up, to cover the cost of the building, publicity, invitations, catering etc.

Izzy left the building and followed a group of tourists down the street. A block later, she entered a small cafe and ordered a coffee, and once she found a seat, she called Amelia.

"Hey! So how's the big city?"

Amelia's excitement transferred over the phone and Izzy smiled automatically. "It's good. Crowded. Bright," she said, looking out at the sunshine glaring off of the glass across from her. "How's the baby mama?"

"We're fine. Just missing the days when I could put on my own shoes—or see them."

Izzy laughed at the comment and fiddled with the cover on her cup.

"Iz? What's going on? Are you okay?"

Izzy turned her attention to the people passing by outside the windows and shook her head, even though Amelia couldn't see it.

"Oh, no. Talk to me," Amelia urged softly.

"I just... I don't know. I don't know if I belong here."

"Did you and Everett have a fight?"

Izzy inhaled and moaned softly. "No. That's just it. He's...wonderful. I can't even complain about him because he's been so amazing. He's been the perfect gentleman," she said. Except when he wasn't such a gentleman—not that she was complaining about *that*.

"So what makes you say you don't belong?"

Izzy closed her eyes and pinched the bridge of her nose. "I guess... It's just the differences in our financial status, you know?"

"Has he said something to make you think it's an issue?"

"No, but..." She explained the offer for a show-case as well as the additional requests. "If the gallery does it, I won't make nearly as much even though I'm doing the work. But if I can front it myself, I could have a really solid return from this."

"Okay, well, if it's that, you know I can front you the money. You don't have to ask Everett. Or your parents. Then you just return whatever doesn't sell."

"I know you'd do that for me, and I thank you for offering. You have no idea how much it means to me but...it just got me thinking."

"Scary words, there, Iz."

Izzy smirked and shook her head again.

"Thinking about what?" Amelia asked.

"Wondering what on earth I have to offer a man like him."

"Oh, *Izzy*. We talked about this."

"I know but I can't help it," she said, lowering her voice. "All of this started as a mistake, but there are times when I feel like he's *bought* me because he has all the connections and I'm just...me."

"*You* are a beautiful, creative, wonderful person who shouldn't be putting herself down," Amelia said.

"I know but wouldn't you wonder?"

"Wonder what?" Amelia asked.

"If that's all it is? If you were me, wouldn't you wonder if you're just some arm candy for the events he doesn't want to attend alone? A project he's amusing himself with for entertainment?"

"Izzy, one—and I'm going to be blunt here—Everett could have any arm candy he wanted. But he didn't ask them. He asked *you*. And as to you being a project...where is all of this coming from? You knew before you left what the arrangement was and you agreed to it."

"I know."

"You'd accompany him and get to know him, and he'd introduce you to the people he knew in the art world."

"I *know* but—"

"But what? What is going on in that crazy brain of yours? What's happened to send you into a spiral of wondering whether or not you're worth someone's time and energy— Oooooh."

Izzy winced. "Yup," she said, knowing Amelia had finally caught on to the fact that she and Everett had taken things to an intimate level yet again.

"You've fallen in love with him, haven't you? That's why you're freaking out?"

It was. They still hadn't known each other long. A matter of weeks. Ms. Georgia had always told them how she'd known right away that she'd met Mr. Right. And while Izzy would totally admit to attraction, hard-core *like*, was it love? "It's too soon. That would be crazy."

"Life's crazy, Iz."

Silence followed Amelia's statement but Izzy had no comment. She stared outside the window, her coffee untouched in front of her.

"Pros and cons. He's wealthy."

"Con."

"Con?"

"And a pro. I mean, it's great that he isn't scraping by like me, but that *really* makes things one-sided here."

"He's handsome."

"Pro," she muttered, unable to deny the fact she found Everett mega-hot.

"He totally seems to like you or he would've just

signed the divorce papers and been done with it already."

"He sees it as failure...and"—she lowered her voice even more—"I can't help but wonder if it's because I didn't sign a prenup since, you know, it was supposed to be fake."

"Honey, a man with that much money doesn't blink at what a court might award you, which probably wouldn't be much since you haven't even made it six months."

"I know, but—"

"You're scared."

Izzy swiped a knuckle beneath her eye and sniffed, blaming the cold seeping in from outside. "It's overwhelming. Like seriously overwhelming."

"Totally understandable. So just take it a day at a time. An hour at a time if you have to."

"It's not that easy. I feel so torn. Between Everett and home and my art and *every*thing."

"Have you talked to him about your feelings?"

"Considering they kinda came out of left field while sitting here, no."

Amelia's smile could be heard in her voice.

"Okay, think of it this way—where do you see yourself in a year? With Everett...or not?"

Her gaze locked on a man across the street. His size and build reminded her of Everett's, and Izzy trained her gaze on him until she couldn't see him any longer.

"Iz? Tick-tock. Gut reaction, come on. With...or without?"

TESSA LEFT THE LADIES' room and reentered the hotel lobby to go back to the ballrooms. The entire conference area had been expanded for the Vegas-style fundraiser. The makeshift casino had tables and slot machines galore, and although the evening was almost over, it was time for the silent auction.

On behalf of her staff, she'd given away a full spa day with nothing excluded, and she couldn't wait to see the happy winner.

She moved through the open doorway, spotting Mary Elizabeth and Adam across the way at the blackjack table. Adaline and her husband were beside them, and all looked to be having a fun time.

Cheryl and her husband had just left to take Ms. Georgia home. The elderly woman had won several hundred dollars, which she had donated back to the toy drive for the local children.

"You look beautiful, Tessie."

She exhaled shakily before pasting on a smile and turning to face Bruce. Her ex-husband looked quite handsome in his suit and tie. "You cleaned up nice yourself."

He seemed surprised by the compliment. But not

nearly as much as she was for giving it. Would the awkwardness ever go away?

"There you are. I've been looking all over for you."

Kirk dragged her close and pressed a kiss to her lips. She didn't even have time to react before it was over, but when she discreetly glanced at Bruce, he glared at Kirk. "I'm right here. Um, Bruce Ridgeway, this is Kirk DeLucca."

Kirk released her long enough to hold out his hand for Bruce to shake. Bruce's reluctance was obvious in his hesitation, but finally he lifted his hand and nodded.

"Kirk."

Kirk's arm wrapped around her once more, and she felt her face heat in embarrassment. She could tell Kirk had had more than a few drinks. He reeked of them, actually. "You know, I'm tired. I think I should be heading home. Bruce, it was nice seeing you."

Kirk held his almost empty glass with his lips and teeth and dug around in his pockets, finding his keys.

"Here we go."

"You're driving?" Bruce asked.

Tessa stiffened and turned back to face the men.

"It's not far."

She winced at the slur in Bruce's words. "I'll drive," she stated pointedly, holding out her hand for the keys.

"Maybe you should let Kirk get a cab," Bruce said.

Tessa noted the way Bruce gave Kirk his best cop's stare, and her grip on the keys tightened. "I'm driving. Good night, Bruce. Kirk, let's go."

The scowl on Bruce's face should've given her some satisfaction except for the fact Kirk had embarrassed her in front of Bruce, and earlier in front of her friends. This was a side of Kirk she hadn't seen and, honestly, didn't like.

"Lead the way, baby. Lead the way," Kirk said, giving Bruce a salacious wink. "We got more to do before the night's over, eh?"

Tessa dug her fingers into Kirk's waist and pulled him along, uncaring that she probably left nail marks as a result.

The moment they were out of sight, she lowered her arm and let him stumble along beside her, all the way through the lobby and outside. Thankfully they didn't have to use the valet line, and she led the way along the side of the hotel to the back of the building, unlocking his Mercedes with a press of the key fob in her hand. "Get in."

"What? No, no. Nobody drives my car but me."

"You just heard me say I'm driving." She losing patience, fast.

"I thought that was just for what's-his-face. I'm fine. Gimme the keysz."

The slur had thickened even more. "No. Either I

drive you or you take an Uber or something. You're in no shape to drive."

Kirk pouted but finally sighed and yanked open the passenger-side door.

"Fine. You drive...and I'll keep celebrating."

For the first time, she noticed the glass he still carried and shook her head. "Leave that here."

"Why're you being so mean?" he slurred. "We're celebrating my project, remember?"

"I remember. But did it require you getting drunk around my friends?"

"Ahh, baby. Don't be mad. Come 'ere."

He shuffled toward her and pulled her against him, lowering his head for a sloppy kiss.

"Kirk, no. I don't like this side of you."

"Now don't be like that. A man's gotta have a little fun, especially when it comes to taking a woman like you to bed."

"*Excuse me?*"

Kirk wiped a hand over his face and rubbed hard.

"Sh—Sorry. I didn't mean that the way it...the way it sounded."

"And how, exactly, did you mean it?"

"I didn't mean nothing. Come on, baby. I'm sorry. I guess I am a little drunker than I thought. Let's go home."

She swallowed hard, and maybe it was the crisp night air or the fact she'd heard a little too much out of Kirk in the last hour or so, but she wanted answers while Kirk was drunk and his tongue was loose. "Tell me what you meant. You said I was beautiful."

"You are for a woman your age. I mean, you haven't let yourself go too much, you know?"

A sharp gasp was all she could manage. Rage rolled over her, and she fisted her hands, the key fob biting into her. "I want my money back," she told him. "I want nothing to do with a project run by someone like you."

"What? Baby—"

"I mean it. How dare you?"

"That money's mine now," he said, the lights from the hotel revealing the ruddy hue of his face. "You gave it to me."

"I mistakenly invested in a company I no longer believe in."

"Because I'm drunk? You can't hold me respons'ble for that."

"Can't I?" She pulled out her phone and scrolled through her contacts, desperately trying to find Tina's number. One thing about owning the most popular salon on the island, she knew people—including the bank manager. She'd done Tina's hair for years.

Tessa hit dial and turned to stalk away only to have Kirk grab her arm and try to yank her back. Tessa heard Tina answer with a low hello and quickly explained she needed an emergency stop payment on a fifty-thousand-dollar check.

Kirk started swearing, his voice growing louder and angrier with every second that passed.

"Tessa? Hon, are you okay? What's going on? Who is that man?"

"Please, Tee, just stop payment. It's urgent."

"Yeah, yeah, I got it. I'll do it right now."

"Thank you."

Kirk released a roar that sent a shiver of fear down her spine, and she hurried to end the call in the hopes that Tina hadn't heard the man.

They were in the back of the hotel, away from most everyone. She twisted her head to look around and didn't see anyone to call for help.

"You little b—"

"Ow! Let me go! Kirk, no!"

Kirk grabbed both her arms and slammed her back against his car, his breath foul when he breathed curses into her face.

"You're not backing out on me."

She lifted her chin and ignored the trembling in her body. "I just did. Now let me go before you get in more trouble and wind up arrested for assault." She tried to remove herself from his grip, but it tightened to the point she cried out in pain again.

"Give me my money."

"Your money? Are you serious?"

"Step away from her."

Tessa closed her eyes for a second before blinking them open again. Of all people to come to her rescue, why did it have to be Bruce?

"This is a private conversation," Kirk said to Bruce, not even bothering to look at him.

Tessa swallowed hard, noting the fact Kirk gripped her so tightly her hands were going numb against his chest. "Kirk, let go and go home."

Calm. She tried to stay calm because screaming and yelling would only escalate the problem, right? She didn't want to make any more of a scene than they already had.

"Call back and undo what you did. Fix it!"

Spittle landed on her cheek from his words, and she flinched back about the same moment Bruce took a step closer, gun drawn.

"Let her go."

Kirk's curses echoed off the building, so loud the surf behind them couldn't drown them out. He shoved her sideways, releasing her so fast she stumbled and fell hard onto the asphalt.

Bruce yelled for Kirk to stop, but Kirk stumbled away, breaking into a run as he disappeared into an alley nearby.

"Tessie? *Tessie?*"

"I'm fine."

"Stay here."

"No!" She stared up at Bruce, panic shooting

through her. "Don't go after him. Please. Stay with me. Don't leave me."

Bruce looked torn between his desire to give chase and heed her words. A second passed, and he pulled his phone from his pocket, hitting a number. Someone answered immediately, and Bruce gave a description of Kirk and the direction he'd headed. "Assault," she heard him say. "I'll add more later."

Tessa sank onto the asphalt, tears rolling down her cheeks. How stupid could she be? How dumb?

"Tessa?"

She shook her head, throat too swollen with tears to speak.

Bruce squatted down next to her and placed a gentle hand on her trembling shoulder.

"It'll be all right, Tessie. I won't let anything happen to you."

The first sob emerged before she could stop it.

"Can you stand? Do you need EMS?"

"No." The word emerged raw and unfiltered. Horrified at the thought of even more people seeing her like this and asking questions she didn't want to answer. "Please. Please, just take me home. I want to go home."

"You should probably get checked out."

She shook her head and forced herself to her feet, ignoring her weak legs and the fact she wanted to vomit. "I want to go home. Take me home o-or I'll take myself."

"There's my girl," Bruce murmured. "Come on then. Let's go."

Neither said a word on the drive home. Tessa stared out the window and fought back tears, desperate to get inside behind closed doors before letting the dam burst.

Foolish. She'd been so very foolish. How could she ever face everyone?

Ten minutes later, Bruce pulled to a stop in her driveway, and even though she tried to escape his presence without another word, he got out when she did and walked her to the door.

"Are you sure you're all right? I have buddies at the fire station. I could get one of the EMTs to come over and take a look."

"I'm fine." Mortified, humiliated, but fine.

"Tessie—"

"Don't. Please. Just...I know, okay? I know everything you're about to say and I've already said it to myself, so just please, let's not."

"You don't have a clue what I'm about to say," Bruce said, voice thick with emotion. "If you did—"

He broke off and she forced her gaze up, found his gaze locked on her, ever watchful. Caring? She blinked, sure she misread it. "If I did?"

His barrel chest lifted and lowered several times as he breathed and a war was fought on his face. Anger, frustration, desire?

"Then you'd know I never stopped loving you,"

he said finally. "After all of these years I-I... Good night, Tessie."

Before she could utter a single word, Bruce turned on his heel and left the porch, striding away so fast she never would've guessed him to be a man in his sixties over one much younger.

He got in the still-running car and backed out of the driveway, headlights swinging over her as he turned. She couldn't see him now. Didn't know if he watched her the way she watched him. But she lifted her hand anyway and waved a silent goodbye.

CHAPTER SIXTEEN

I can't believe it. Give Tessa my best and tell her I hope she feels better soon," Izzy said before murmuring a goodbye to her mama and ending the call.

"Bad news?"

Izzy turned and found Everett leaning against the doorway of the living room, one foot crossed over the front at his ankle. He looked gorgeous and casual and... "How long have you been there?"

The smile that lifted his lips made her belly flutter.

"A while. Just enjoying the view."

His gaze swept over her and left her insides heating in a way that couldn't happen. Not today. "Mmm, um, yes, actually that was bad news. Tessa was involved in something. I didn't grasp the whole story, but she'll be okay. That's the important thing."

"Good."

"Yeah. So...we have things to do, and since you insist on joining me in tackling the chaos, are you ready?"

She'd discussed the different opportunities for gallery shows with Everett, but when it came down to it, she was most interested in the one where she could showcase her art the way she would want it displayed, surrounded by things that complimented the colors and lines and shapes of the frames. Maybe it was the control freak in her, but she couldn't think of anything more fun than staging it all and watching everyone's reactions.

Everett insisted she choose that one, promising to provide whatever she wanted, and he'd seemed genuinely surprised when she refused his offer. Thanks to Amelia, Izzy wouldn't be beholden to Everett for the expense of the endeavor, and she wanted to keep it that way. With the gallery providing catering and the staff to help with pricing and purchasing the night of the event, she couldn't help but get her hopes up for a successful evening.

"Let's go," he said.

Moments later they left the underground garage and made their way to Saks first. The problem was it was Christmastime...in New York, and the store was teeming with people.

Smiling at her, Everett drew her off to the side and watched as she pulled out her iPad. She'd made a long list of potential items to go with the photos, and she intended to enjoy every bit of this shopping spree, people included, even if she didn't get to keep any of the items.

"So what's first?" Everett asked.

A giggle burst out of her before she could stop it. "Lingerie." Her smile widened when his eyebrows rose. "What? Surely you've purchased lingerie for your lady friends?"

"I have...not," he said, dipping his head to stare down at her much shorter form. "But you can bet I'll pay close attention to your selections while we're here."

Everett's gaze set her body on fire, and she cleared her throat and followed the signs for the department she needed. One thing was certain—she had Everett's full attention now. And she intended to make the most of it.

HOURS AND HOURS LATER, Izzy fell into the package-crowded backseat of the car and scooted over for Everett to join her. The moment he settled, he pulled her lower legs atop his and gently began to massage her through her leggings. Izzy couldn't stop the groan that formed.

"I thought if mine were hurting in comfortable shoes, yours must be killing you," he murmured.

"Have mercy," she breathed, gasping when he pressed and rubbed a particularly tender muscle.

The chuckle that emerged from his chest drew her lashes up and she wondered when she'd shut them.

"Feel good?"

"Heavenly."

"Dinner in tonight?"

"Oh, please." She didn't want to think about anything but a long, hot bath and cozy socks. The boots she'd worn had always been favorites due to being comfortable, but after spending the entire day and most of the evening traipsing through stores and boutiques, she was stick-a-fork-in-her done.

She shifted on the leather seat and curled her arm through Everett's to lean her head against his shoulder while Tomas drove them home.

"You scored some amazing things for your New York debut," Everett said, the words whispered into her hair. "You have good taste, Isabel."

"Thank you." The compliment meant a lot. It really did. Her taste was definitely different from her mother's more traditional style. Isabel had a very modern, minimalist style. She'd focused on textures and shapes and tried to keep things as elegant yet homey as possible. The end result would be clean and warm, cozy yet rich.

"I can't wait to see it all set up."

She tipped her head back to better see him. "So you weren't bored today?"

"With you? Never."

Sweet words from a man who knew how to wield them. "Careful there or you'll make me think you're smitten."

The words emerged and she waited for Everett's response, but he merely smiled and turned his head to stare out the window.

Okay, then.

Forcing her thoughts away from the man beside her, she focused on the purchases she'd made today. The bigger items would be delivered to the gallery for the showcase, but the smaller ones like jewelry and clothing were packed into the car with them. Margo had said to keep the numbers low, so that the items would be thought of as more exclusive and more likely to be chosen before they disappeared. "I can't thank you enough," she said, breaking the silence. "Those boutiques you took me to were the cherry on top."

"You can thank Jacob when you see him next. He put out a few inquiries and came up with them."

"I will." Those were her favorite stores, the smaller ones a little out of the way but so worth the effort of finding them. Poor Tomas had to handle the traffic getting them there, but she was thrilled with how successful the day had turned out. "Thank you. For letting them use the painting I gave you."

"Of course."

"And for getting another watch to display. I have a feeling it will sell fast, seeing as how it's on that sexy arm I painted."

She felt his lips brush against her hair and her spine tingled.

"Sexy arm," he repeated, "wrapped around a sexy woman."

His statement reminded her of her conversation with Amelia. Izzy leaned her head back once more, staring up at his angled, five-o'clock-shadowed jawline while he looked out the window.

Was that all she was to him? A pretty face? Oh, she was sure he could find more attractive women for arm candy, but convenience had to play a part. With Everett not wanting his mistake made public for the gossip rags, he was kind of stuck with her.

She inhaled and straightened at the unattractive thought, shifting away from his body and the temptation it posed. It was all too easy to lean against him, breathe in his scent, and pretend everything was okay. And it was—on the surface.

But beneath the chummed water, the sharks circled.

How long did he intend to pretend? It wasn't like their appearances together all over town hadn't caused a bit of a stir. She'd seen the photos on the internet and in the tabloids as they walked the streets of the city. She was a nobody but Everett...Everett wasn't. That meant they were on a lot of people's radar. How long until they started digging into their relationship and how it had begun? How long before their secret went public?

Tomas pulled into the parking garage, and Everett asked him to take the many bags and boxes to the gallery next since they'd be staying in for the evening.

Everett stepped from the car, stretching out a hand to help her before accepting several bags Tomas pulled from the front seat.

"Thank you for driving us, Tomas."

"My pleasure, Ms. Shipley."

The elevator arrived promptly, and Izzy eyed the packages Everett held with narrow-eyed suspicion. "Christmas gifts for your staff?"

Amusement made his eyes twinkle.

"No."

"I hope those aren't for me." Unease filled her. She didn't have the money to be buying expensive gifts.

"And if they are?"

"Everett, you've already done more than enough. I can't possibly accept anything else."

The elevator doors opened and he tilted his head, indicating she should go first. "Good thing I didn't ask you then. And you did give me something for Christmas—the painting."

"Created from the studio you gifted me."

"Isabel," he said softly, lowering the bags to the floor and moving to stand in front of her. He took hold of her coat, clenching her lapels in his big hands. "This isn't a competition."

"I know but—"

"But nothing. I want to spoil you. Let me."

Christmas was only a few days away now, and even though Everett had offered to fly her back to Carolina Cove for Christmas, the showcase was two days after Christmas, and she had too much to do to prepare. She'd informed her family, and they'd all agreed that Christmas was when they were together, not a date, so they'd celebrate after her return, when she'd be home for their annual New Year's Eve party. "I just wish... What do I get the man who has everything?"

He lowered his head and kissed her. "I can think of some things," he said against her lips, moving to her ear to whisper them.

CHRISTMAS CAME AND WENT. Everett had purchased several things for Isabel to have under the tree come Christmas morning, focusing on items she might find endearing rather than over-the-top.

During their shopping trip, he'd noticed her eyeing several sketchbooks but choosing instead a more common notebook for the showcase. While she went on shopping, he'd purchased a leather-bound sketchbook, set of watercolor pencils, as well as a platinum charm bracelet featuring an artist palette. To that he'd added a palm tree and Las Vegas charm, along with an apple for New York. And last but not least, he'd carefully selected and purchased a negligee, a silvery-emerald color that made her eyes pop and brought all sorts of ideas to mind.

His gaze shifted to the small, framed portrait across from him on the mantel. Isabel had gifted him with a painting of him and his mother. It was a favorite photo kept on his bedside table, one she'd noticed and copied. His heart squeezed when he looked at it, noting Isabel's extreme talent for depicting emotions with paint. His mother's head was tilted back, eyes sparkling and half-closed as she laughed. He was on her lap, looking up at her with all the love a boy has for his mother.

The painting was now one of his most prized possessions. That and the portrait of Isabel in his arms.

A knock sounded on his home office door, but before he called out, the panel opened and his father stepped through.

"There's my boy. Jacob let me in."

Everett grinned and stood to accept his father's hug. "How are you? How was the honeymoon?"

"Ah, well, you know how things go."

Everett's gut clenched as he took a step back and

returned to his seat, watching warily as his father paced across the room to the bar on the far side of his office. "It's a little early for that, isn't it?"

His father ignored Everett's question and poured a double. "Dad? What's going on?"

James Everett Sr. sucked back half the drink before answering.

"I really thought she was it."

Everett grimaced and covered his curse with his hand. "What happened?"

"The pool boy. That's what happened," his father growled.

Yeah, well, considering she was twenty-three to his sixty-seven, could he really be surprised? "I'm sorry to hear that."

"Onward. Right, my boy?"

If that meant the next woman, Everett sincerely hoped not.

"So what have you been into while I've been gone? Did I see you in the papers with a woman on your arm? Normally you're careful not to let that happen. Gives 'em too many ideas."

Everett shifted in his chair and sat forward, bracing his elbows on the desk in front of him. His father's statement was true. In the past, he was careful to keep his private life private. He attended social events alone, choosing to go solo rather than have his date think too much of the invitation and attention. "Her name is Isabel. She's an artist."

"Ahhh, that explains it. You found yourself a Dharma to your Greg."

The reference to the old television show did nothing to soothe Everett's mood. He had a couple days left before Isabel's return to Carolina Cove for the holidays, and he wasn't sure how he felt about it. Things had been going well with them. Well enough that she hadn't mentioned their divorce for a week. "If you say so," he said simply. "So things are in motion for divorce number eight?"

"Yeah. I guess there's just no replacing your mother."

Everett stiffened and sat back in his leather chair. "Maybe you shouldn't compare them—and find someone your own age."

His father's loud chuckle echoed throughout the room. "Women my age have too many issues and make me think about my own. It's the young ones that make you forget," James said with a wink.

Recognizing a losing battle when he saw it, Everett shrugged. "I hate to cut this short but I have a meeting in a bit." The meeting was him going to where Isabel's showcase would be held to help her any way he could, but he didn't want to tell his father that and have him ask to tag along. "Did you need something?"

"Nah, just checking in now that I'm back. Maybe we can have dinner tonight so I can meet your lady friend."

"She's busy preparing for a show." When his father looked at him expectantly, Everett added, "It's tomorrow evening. I'll have Jacob send you an invitation."

"Wonderful."

His father finished his drink and stood. Everett did as well, walking the man to the door. On the way, his father paused and stared at the mantel.

"That's new."

Everett stiffened. "It was my Christmas present from Isabel."

"I see."

"I can see if she would paint another if you like," he offered, unwilling to give up the gift that meant so much to him.

His father ran a hand over his face, never taking his gaze off the portrait.

"Yeah. Yeah, I'd like that."

Seconds more passed with his father staring at the photo before James yanked open the door and left.

Everett's gaze met Jacob's and he made the request for the invitation.

That done, his father moved toward the elevator while Everett reentered his office, his mood darkened by his father's eighth failed attempt to find happiness. Everett knew his father's choices were highly to blame, but it was another notch on the divorce belt.

"Sir? Tomas has the car out front whenever

SEASCAPES AND VEGAS MISTAKES   273

you're ready," Jacob said. He held out a packet. "And these just arrived for you from your attorney."

Everett took the envelope and opened it on his way back into his office. The paperwork was short and straightforward, requiring only signatures and a few initials.

He glared at the papers, stomach knotted. This wasn't how he wanted to start the new year.

But how could he convince her to stay?

"SO, have they put a stop on the check?" Mary Elizabeth asked while pouring Tessa a cup of tea.

"Yes, it's taken care of." As always, mortification filled her when she thought of how close she'd been to losing her savings to a scam artist. How *stupid* she'd been.

"Come on, Tessa. Everyone makes mistakes. You have to forgive yourself."

"I can't," she whispered, stirring sugar into her tea. "I can't believe I allowed myself to be taken in by him. I mean, you were right. He was so young. Why would any man that young be interested in an old woman except for money?"

"Stop. You might have been older than him, but he targeted you because you're beautiful and successful."

"And stupid," she muttered again.

"Okay, that's it. You have five more minutes to rant about this before you're going to suck it up, drop it, and not focus on it anymore. It happened. You've learned a valuable lesson. Now let's move on."

Five minutes to vent over something that was sixty-three years in the making? She should've known better! "I just hate how easy it was for him to get to me."

"Con men are smooth talkers. They know how to groom you, Tessa. You aren't the first woman to be taken in by them and you won't be the last."

"At least he's in jail." Bruce's buddies on the force had found Kirk trying to blend in with the crowd on the boardwalk. "Well, I'm done. I give up. I've had my share of men and marriage and...no more. Ever."

"Uh-huh," Mary Elizabeth said, a doubting look on her face. "Just give it time and stop trying to make it happen. When you stop forcing things...that's when you'll meet someone."

The phone rang and Mary Elizabeth picked it up. "Hello? Oh, Everett. How are you?"

Mary Elizabeth met Tessa's gaze, eyes widening and mouth turning into a small O of surprise.

"I see. Yes, of course. Thank you for calling... Yes, yes, I'll be sure to let them know. Tomorrow morning, ten o'clock," she said before listening again and then murmuring goodbye.

"What was that about?" Tessa asked the moment Mary Elizabeth hung up the phone.

"That was Everett," Mary Elizabeth said needlessly, "inviting us to Isabel's showcase. He said he knew getting airfare at the last minute could be problematic, so he's sending his jet to pick up anyone who'd like to go."

"Wow. Really?" She'd hated to miss Isabel's first New York City art show, but given everything that had happened with Kirk, she hadn't been in the mood to deal with booking a flight and fighting the holiday crowds.

Mary Elizabeth picked up her cell phone, and Tessa watched as she typed out a message. A second later, her phone dinged with Everett's invitation and details.

"Does this mean things between them are serious?" Tessa asked.

"I couldn't tell you. I've barely spoken to her since they went to New York. She's texted to say she's painting and exploring the city, but she hasn't mentioned how things are going with them and...I haven't asked."

"That's not like you," Tessa teased. "Why not?"

Mary Elizabeth reached up and ran her fingertips over the diamond cross at her neck.

"Any time I approve of something, that girl runs in the opposite direction. This time? I'm praying for God's hand over my mouth and a man who loves my daughter enough to support her during those times when she isn't able to support herself."

"Ouch."

"I know. It's awful to hear myself say it but it's true. I pray this showcase works out for her. That Everett works out for her."

"Well, as I'm proof, there are worse things than being alone, MeMe. Trust me."

"But you're not alone. You have the Babes...and Bruce?"

Just the mention of his name sent a shiver through her. "I do not have Bruce."

"He seemed awfully protective of you that night."

"His whole job is to protect and serve."

"This was different and you know it. Are you sure—"

"Yes! I'm sure. I'm quite sure I'll never be able to show my face to him again because I'm so embarrassed."

"Oh, Tessa."

"I mean it. It's bad enough that you girls know what happened, but Bruce *witnessed it.*"

"So? Maybe it was an eye opener for him, too?"

"How?" Tessa asked.

Mary Elizabeth grinned. "Tessa, for such a worldly woman, you're blinded when it comes to Bruce. The man still loves you. He's never stopped."

The statement reminded Tessa of Bruce's words that night, leaving her stomach in knots. "That's... hard to believe."

"It shouldn't be."

Tessa shoved her fingers through her short hair and then smoothed it down. "How is that possible? After all these years?"

"It's possible for the same reason you still love him," Mary Elizabeth said.

"I don't—"

"You do. Oh, Tessa, saying you don't love that man is like saying Isabel isn't an artist. Who's lying to themselves about reality now?"

CHAPTER SEVENTEEN

The warehouse couldn't have been more perfect for the showcase.

Isabel stared up at the twinkle lights hanging from the wood and metal beams, feeling a bit out of body due to the beauty of it all.

The warehouse's brick and metal structure highlighted the earthy tones she favored in her work, and with the addition of the many pieces she'd curated to accompany her art, she felt like she'd stepped into another world.

One side of the warehouse featured her coastal paintings—curtesy of Everett and his private jet that had also brought her parents and several of the Babes.

"Izzy?"

She turned at the sound of her name and gasped

when her pseudo-cousin Devon stepped close for a hug.

Devon was the host of *What's Hot*, and she'd jumped on the uniqueness of the rave-type showcase. "Look at you! Girl, can you stop it with the gorgeousness?" Izzy said.

Devon laughed and shook her head, hugging her again. "Right back at you. This is *amazing*. I knew it would be great but...everything is perfect! The paintings, the design aspects. You walk into other worlds with each setup."

"It did turn out pretty great, yeah?"

"Her hard work has paid off," Everett said, joining them.

Izzy made the introductions and watched as her lifelong friend sized up the man at her side.

"It's nice to meet you, Mr. Drake."

"Everett, please. I've watched your show many times, Devon. I look forward to seeing Isabel's art featured soon."

Izzy watched as her cousin's eyes sparkled and a perfectly plucked eyebrow rose when Everett wrapped his arm around her shoulders and pulled her to his side.

"I look forward to showing it," Devon said, shooting Izzy a knowing glance.

"Leave it to my boy to be surrounded by beautiful women."

Izzy turned in unison with Everett to see a much older version of Everett watching them.

"Isabel, this is my father, James. Dad, Isabel Shipley and her cousin Devon."

Izzy smiled when the older man immediately flirted with both her and Devon, all the while eyeing an attractive woman nearby.

Okay, then. Now the many marriages were explained.

Everett had mentioned his father was now on divorce number eight, and she pitied the man. To marry that many times only to divorce... It made her sad to think about it. But given the man's wandering eye, she instinctively knew he searched for something he'd lost when Everett's mother had passed.

Why did some people find happiness while others didn't? Couldn't? She wasn't one of those people who believed in soul mates, because the odds of finding one person in the entire world seemed ridiculous. But finding one of the many compatible people to make a life with seemed just as difficult as finding that one.

She still pondered the question of love in the wee hours of the morning when the warehouse cleared and the showcase ended.

The majority of the smaller items had been sold and taken home with their purchasers, and larger items awaiting delivery were marked as sold.

She took a slow tour through the warehouse,

aghast at the sight of so many sold tags. Her hand trembled as she pressed her fingertips to her mouth. If she wasn't mistaken, she stood at a good ninety to ninety-five percent. Unbelievable!

She'd done it. She'd actually done it! Even the watch had sold, with orders for two more. All because they'd staged it as a bedroom scene with the painting above a dresser, the watch displayed atop. "Unbelievable."

She'd get commissions on those sales, too.

"Isabel? Are you ready to head home?" Everett asked.

Home. She turned to face him and wound up running the two steps to plaster herself against him. "Thank you."

He kissed her briefly, softly. "You're welcome. Margo said the gallery is thrilled. You sold out, sweetheart."

"Not quite but almost, yeah. I can't believe it."

The air left her lungs and she blinked hard, earning another kiss from Everett.

"Don't look so surprised. I knew you could do it."

The words warmed her even more as Everett led her to the exit.

She sat in the backseat of the car with Everett while Tomas drove them to the penthouse. It felt a little strange staying with Everett rather than with her parents at the hotel before their return to

Carolina Cove tomorrow—er, today? The sun would be rising in a matter of hours.

"Happy?" Everett asked.

"Yes."

And exhausted. She'd worked nonstop to make sure the showcase was perfect, fussing over every detail.

They made their way through the penthouse to Everett's bedroom—the one they'd shared after that first night.

Everett lowered his head and kissed her, then swung her up into his arms to carry her inside to his bed.

Izzy pressed her lips to his, fingers digging into his hair. "I love you," she whispered softly.

Everett lowered his head and kissed her again.

HOURS LATER IZZY LEFT EVERETT sleeping and made her way through the penthouse. Exhaustion pulled at her, but she was too restless to sleep, especially with the sun on the rise and so many unanswered questions in her heart.

She and Everett had made love and she'd *said*... But he hadn't said it back. He'd simply gazed at her and then kissed her so passionately he stole her breath and whatever might have remained protected in her heart.

A now shattered heart because, through it all, why hadn't he said it back?

Izzy padded barefoot through the penthouse, taking in the sights and sounds along the way. She found herself outside of his office door, the scent of leather and sandalwood strong. Izzy pushed open the paneled door and took in the masculine interior, sealing it in her memory.

The small portrait of Everett and his mother sat front and center on the mantel. She stared at the piece, running her fingertips over Everett's little-boy face, her heart tugging with emotions she refused to welcome.

When she looked at Everett, she could imagine so many things. A future. A family?

But then again, how could she want more from a man unable to give her the one thing she needed most?

She noted a dark navy throw over the back of the couch and headed in that direction, hoping to ease the chill in the room. Along the way, she spotted an envelope on the desk addressed to both Everett and herself.

Her heart thudded hard in her chest as she moved the envelope off the top of the pages. Their divorce papers?

Simple, to the point—except for one thing. She shook her head, eyes widening as she read the spousal support she would receive. She'd never asked

Everett for money, and she didn't intend to do so now. It wasn't like they'd been married twenty years and had children together. A month give or take didn't qualify for that kind of support, even if he was a billionaire.

Her hands shook as she found a pen and crossed out that section, initialing it at the side. That done, she flipped to the signature page and hesitated only a moment before adding her name through eyes glazed by tears.

Everett was a wonderful man. Kind, obviously generous. But she needed the words, and if all he had to offer her was his money...she needed to protect herself.

She needed more than sex and the pretense of being married. She wanted it all or nothing at all. His choice.

She dashed her knuckles under her eyes when tears threatened to spill and forced her chin high. She was exhausted, overly emotional, and now...realizing she'd face the new year alone while the man she loved remained distant.

Still, she'd rather be alone than be in a relationship with someone who didn't love her. Couldn't love her because he was too afraid of being hurt. Love was a risk. It was wonderful and painful and blissful. Beautiful even though it was oftentimes full of tears.

But she wanted it, *needed* it. She deserved to have the man she loved love her in return.

She capped the pen and set it atop the papers before sniffling and hurrying through the door. In her bedroom, she got dressed in seconds, packed in minutes, and texted her parents that she would meet them at the airport. To not leave without her.

Finally her taxi made it there, and even though she knew she looked awful, she couldn't help it. She rushed up the steps of the private plane, her only bag on her shoulder. She'd send for the rest later and pray Amelia would forgive her for leaving so many of her clothes behind.

"She's here," her father said to a man in a pilot's uniform. "We can take off now."

"I'm sorry, sir. We'll be delayed a bit longer due to weather," the man said.

"Izzy? Are you okay?" her mama asked.

Izzy tried to keep it together. She tried *hard*. But staring at the faces watching her so lovingly, with so much concern... She burst into tears and couldn't stop.

Tessa made it to her first, surrounding her with a hug that was quickly piled on as the ladies on board did what mothers do under such circumstances.

"Oh, honey, what happened? Surely it can't be that bad," Tessa asked, tears thickening her voice as she cried in sympathy.

"Sweetheart?"

Hearing her daddy's voice made things worse. She sobbed harder, knowing once again she'd disappointed everyone. But especially him. Her father had liked Everett. She could tell. So much so she'd even daydreamed about the two of them watching football together or playing golf.

Like mother hens, the Babes gently pushed, shoved, and manhandled her to the back of the plane, where someone shoved an orange drink in her hand and told her to sip.

Hands patted her, stroked her hair, and tissues appeared out of nowhere.

When she finally calmed down enough to look up, she spotted her father talking to the pilot, his expression grim.

He must have felt her stare because he glanced back at her, nodding in reference to something the pilot said.

"Isabel," her mother said, "what's wrong, honey? I thought you'd be floating on cloud nine today after your showcase. We are so proud of you. Why are you crying? What happened?"

"He doesn't... He doesn't love me."

The words burst out of her, low and full of pain. She hadn't meant to just blurt it out like that, but she had and there it was, hanging in the air in front of all of them.

"What makes you say that?" her mama asked, stroking another tear off her cheek.

"Because I told him. I told him that I love him and he didn't...he didn't say *any*thing," she said, leaving off the part about how Everett had simply taken her to bed. "I-I know I can be difficult and moody sometimes, but I thought he... I thought he *loved* me."

"Oh, honey." Her mama hugged her again.

"Mary Elizabeth, let me," Tessa said. "Izzy, baby, I know he hurt you when he didn't say the words in return, but the man I saw last night is head-over-heels in love with you."

"He's not," she argued, shaking her head as a fresh batch of tears surfaced. "It was just... We were just a business arrangement. He needed a date for his events and h-he introduced me to people from the art world. It was an exchange, that's all," she said, side-stepping the truth a bit by leaving out their marriage. "He bought me like a-a—"

"Now, now, I don't think that's what it was at all," Tessa said. "He couldn't take his eyes off of you."

Izzy wiped her face and shook her head. It was true, all of it. They didn't know it was true, and her life of late was all a lie, but how could it be anything but?

How many times had she told Everett she didn't want his money? Why would he put such a thing in the divorce papers? To ensure her silence? As payment for not disclosing information about him?

Tessa squeezed Izzy's hand before turning it over and fingering the bracelet she hadn't taken off since Everett had fastened it.

"What's this?" her mother asked. "Was it from Everett?"

Izzy swallowed the lump in her throat and forced a nod.

"So the man bought you jewelry, created an art studio *in his house* for you, and helped you with your career...and you don't think he cares for you?" Tessa asked.

"Caring isn't love. Buying me things isn't love." Love was more. So much more. And even though Everett might care for her, she needed more. She needed the words he hadn't said. Words he apparently couldn't say. At least not to her.

"Honey, you know what happened with me recently," Tessa said. "So let me give you another perspective, just to think about. Okay?"

Izzy nodded, willing to accept any and all advice.

"Kirk came on strong, much like your Everett. He flirted and gave me flowers. Charmed me. But it wasn't real. He just wanted money."

"I don't have any money. Everett knows that," she said with a grumble.

"Exactly, sweetheart," Tessa said. "He's done all of those wonderful things for you knowing you don't have the money or the connections to return the gesture. So why did he do it?"

Izzy shot Tessa a stare that made it clear Everett *had* gotten something in return, but the woman only shook her head.

"No. Sweetheart, that is something a man like him can get anywhere. There's more to this story, you mark my words."

She didn't dare hope that was true. She couldn't. "I want to go home. Can we please go home?"

"Soon, miss," the captain said. "Everyone, just relax and have a drink and we'll be on our way soon."

Izzy finally met her mother's stare. Tears swept through her again, blurring her vision. "I'm sorry, Mama. I know I keep disappointing you."

"Oh, Isabel. Honey, you have not disappointed me."

"You liked Everett. You want things to work with him."

"I love you," her mother said softly. "The only thing I want is for you to be happy. Do you hear me?"

EVERETT FOUGHT his impatience as Tomas raced to the airport.

Hands fisting, he stared out the window, his mind rolling over the morning. The bed had been empty when he woke up, so he'd dressed and searched the penthouse for Isabel.

The moment he'd spotted the pen atop the papers his attorney had delivered, a chill had raced down his spine, settling low and deep and making his muscles ache.

He remembered stalking toward the desk, spying Isabel's signature, and scowling at it, the breath leaving his lungs in a painful rush.

How could she do this now? After everything they'd shared? After telling him she loved him?

It took him a moment to realize she'd added a sticky note to the signature page that said, *I'm sorry. I need more.*

More? More what? More money?

He yanked the papers up and flipped to the one regarding the settlement. She'd crossed it out and written in the margin, but where he thought to find a higher amount requested, he read exactly where he could stick his money. With Isabel's initials beside it.

A huff left his chest as he tossed the papers down and ran his fingers through his hair.

She wasn't like the others. Thank God.

But if she thought she was going to just leave without a goodbye...

He grabbed the phone from the desk and dialed his pilot. The moment the man answered, Everett growled, "I think you have an extra passenger on the way—Isabel Shipley. Do not take off and do not let her leave the plane. I'm on my way."

Now they drove, the traffic busy as Tomas floored the car get them there as quickly as he could.

Finally arriving, Everett jumped out of the car

before it had completely stopped and ran across the tarmac to the private plane decked in the Drake Enterprises logo.

He ran up the steps, boarding so fast he heard several gasps of surprise from the ladies on board. And Isabel.

Her eyes widened when she saw him. She'd just exited the rear bathroom, eyes puffy like she'd been crying. Now she stood frozen in place, one hand lifting to rub her chest as her anxiety appeared upon seeing him.

Everett stalked down the aisle, holding her gaze so she wouldn't look away.

"Everett, just stop. I know I should've told you I was leaving but—"

"How much?" he asked, taunting her, desperate and uncaring of the fact as he tested her one last time.

"What?" Her eyes widened even more and she shook her head. "You think I want more *money*?" she asked in a low voice, disappointment crossing her face before turning to disgust. "You jerk, you don't know me at all, do you?"

He grinned at her response. "I do know you. That's why I want you, Isabel."

"If you think you can *buy* me... Oh, I don't believe you! I told you I love you, you screwed up, stupid man, and *that's* what you think I want in return? You're unbelievable!"

She tried to shove past him, but Everett caught her arm in a firm grip and wouldn't let go.

"Izzy? Is everything all right?" her mother asked.

Considering they had a plane full of people watching their every move, Everett fought a surge of embarrassment but pressed on. It couldn't be helped. If it meant baring his soul, he would.

"It's fine, Mom."

"It doesn't look fine," her father added. "Son, you'd be wise to let go of my daughter."

Everett heeded the warning out of respect. But he didn't move out of the way. "Isabel...stay with me."

"I can't."

"Why?"

"Because I need the words."

"I love you."

"Yes, *those* words."

"How about 'be my wife'?"

She blinked at him. "Yes... Wait, what?"

"You heard me."

"Everett, I signed the papers."

He bent his knees until he could look into her gaze. "I don't care. I'll rip them up. We can do this."

"Because of your dad? Fear of failing doesn't make a marriage, Everett."

"Is this about a prenup?" one of the Babes asked in a stage whisper.

"Shhh," said another. "Hush!"

"Because *I love you*, Isabel. I love you, and I don't want to lose you."

"You do—er, don't?"

He shook his head and fought off the urge to curse. "It occurs to me that we might have a communication issue we need to work on."

"I don't understand."

"I know," he whispered, raking his hand through his hair. "But hear me out, okay? The words... Isabel, my father said he loved every woman he's ever met. And then a few days or a week or a month later, there would be another woman, like the words had never been said and meant less."

"They mean everything to me."

"I know. I see that now. But before... I thought you'd understand that me helping you was... I've always been a person who believed actions speak louder than words."

"Told you," Tessa said.

Isabel's mouth dropped open in surprise. "You helped me because...you love me?"

"Yes. And the words do mean something—everything—when they come from you," he said, being brutally honest. "And from now on, they mean the same to me. When I say I love you, I mean it."

She nodded, tears filling her eyes.

"Actions are good," she whispered, "b-but love is meant to be voiced. Seen. Felt. But only if you mean it," she hurried to clarify. "Please don't say it if you don't."

He stepped closer, drawing her into his body and using one hand to gently lift her chin. "I think I fell in love with you the moment I saw you in Vegas. You were standing beneath a spotlight at the gallery, wearing a gold dress, and you looked like something out of a dream."

He heard the sighs from the ladies behind them. If only his words were impacting the woman in front of him as much as the Babes. "I can't imagine my life without you, Isabel. Not because I don't want to fail but because I can't see a future without you in it. Please, stay. We'll figure out the logistics but...be my wife. For real."

A tear trickled from her lashes, and he swiped at it with his thumb, holding her weight as she pressed her hands against his chest and rose to her toes to kiss him.

Behind them the passengers burst into excited squeals and applause, and he felt her smiling against his lips at their enthusiastic response.

"Oh, I have a wedding to plan," her mother said.

"*We* have a wedding to plan," one of the other Babes said.

Everett chuckled and hugged Isabel tight.

"Should we tell them we're already...?" she asked, the words muffled by his shoulder.

"We'll tell them on our twentieth anniversary," he

whispered. "Let them plan. I want to see my bride in a real dress, not a Vegas rental."

She giggled as she drew away from him and leaned back to stare up at him, arms wrapped around his neck.

"You really mean it? You're not just saying it because—"

He kissed her again, and again. "I love you, Isabel. And if you stop running away from me, I'll keep telling you every chance I get."

She laughed again, the sound everything he wanted to hear and more.

I sabel looked around and took in the smiling faces surrounding her. "Ready? One, two..."

The single female guests waited anxiously for the bouquet toss, and Izzy couldn't wait to see the winner.

The crowd cheered when she tossed it over her head. Devon caught it one-handed right before the bouquet would've smacked her in the face, looking surprised and horrified as she tossed it like a hot potato to one of the other cousins.

Izzy laughed at her antics, noting the blush on Devon's pretty face when she sent a glance in a certain direction across the room and slogged back her champagne like a sorority girl.

Izzy followed the stare and raised an eyebrow high when Oz pretended to be as oblivious. Even though he wore the same hot-faced flush that fooled no one.

The neighbor and family friend had grown up with the cousins, and at one point Oz and Devon were engaged to be married. But ever since the breakup, they'd avoided each other, with Devon spending ninety-nine percent of her time in New York. She came home for special occasions, unlike their cousin Hadley who had disappeared off the face of the earth in the past year.

Izzy looked around the room again, frowning when she realized Hadley hadn't attended the reception.

Izzy had received Hadley's response declining her invitation to the wedding with a sweet note of apology, but she'd hoped Hadley would at least make an appearance here.

Izzy worried about Hadley and she knew she wasn't the only one. Cheryl and Ms. Georgia looked concerned where they sat with the Babes across the room, and Izzy tried to remember the last time Hadley had been home for a visit.

Ms. Georgia wasn't getting any younger, and it wasn't like Hadley to stay away so long. Nor could Izzy shake the unease that something was going on to keep Hadley away. But what?

Strong arms slipped around her waist and pulled her flush against a hard body, and Izzy turned her face up to stare at her husband.

Husband.

Even though they'd been married since Vegas, she had to admit planning the wedding had been a blast. She'd felt like a princess in her never-before-worn white wedding gown, and Everett was definitely her handsome prince in his tailor-made gray tuxedo.

"What's got you looking so pensive?"

Izzy shoved her thoughts about Hadley away and focused on this moment. This man. "Mm. I have a *secret*," she whispered, unable to wait a moment longer even though she hadn't planned on telling him until they were alone.

"Oh?"

She grinned up at him and turned in his arms, pulling his head down to whisper in his ear. "Ballsy move of you having Michael draw up house plans without consulting me."

Everett sighed and stroked a thumb over her cheek. "My surprise is ruined? Great."

"Don't blame Michael. I insisted on taking a look."

"Well, the plans are just a draft. You'll get input, trust me."

"Hmm. I'll say. Would you like to see what I've changed?"

"Now?"

Her smile widened as Everett's frown deepened. He undoubtedly knew she was up to something.

"Yes, now. I had Michael make some changes, and," she drawled, glancing across the room to see Michael give her a nod, "they're over there."

She took Everett by the hand and led him to the table where Michael sat. The moment they approached her cousin, Everett's best friend, he lifted his hands in surrender.

"I only did as ordered," Michael said to Everett with a wide grin.

Everett shot her another quizzical glance before looking over the plans now spread across the table. Only one change had been made. One very important one.

She heard the moment Everett saw the addition to her home studio. He sucked in a sharp breath and shoved himself off the table where he'd braced his hands to stare down at the plans. He turned, grabbed her up in his arms, and whirled her around, much to their audience's delight.

"What's going on?"

"Oh! They're building a house," Sophia said to the crowd.

"Where?"

"Here?"

"Oh, Isabel, *really*?" her mother asked, excitement layering her tone.

Izzy stared into Everett's loving gaze, ignoring the comments and questions, to revel in the moment and capture every nuance in case she wanted to paint it later.

They *were* building a house in Carolina Cove— but it was the tiny little nursery room she'd added between her studio and the kitchen that had caught Everett's attention and caused his celebration.

A smile tugged at her lips, matching his, and she lowered her head to kiss him, softly, tenderly. Breathlessly.

Telling Him.

If she ever painted this moment, that's what it would be called.

Are you curious about where cousin Hadley is hiding? Or better yet, *why* she's hiding? Keep reading for a sneak peek at SEASHELLS AND WEDDING BELLS, available for pre-order!

Hadley Masterson pulled to a stop outside the funeral home and prayed for God to strike her dead.

She didn't *want* to die. But dead would be a whole lot easier than walking in that door alone. And once she was inside? She had little chance at escaping unnoticed.

Truth be told, she'd much rather take her chances with a forgiving Maker than her mother.

Was that bad?

She closed her eyes and shook her head at herself. She was a forty-five-year-old woman who quivered in fear at the thought of facing a woman once crowned the island's Mermaid Queen.

Yeah, well, it didn't have to be like this, did it, Haddie? Why did you wait so long? Lie?

She fisted her hands in frustration and tried to mentally find her bootstraps.

What had seemed like a good idea at the time was now a nightmare, and wishes and wants would get her nowhere. When the time was right, she had to break the news. Somehow.

Hadley got out of the car and fought the urge to dive back in and make a break for it while she could. Squealing away from the funeral home like a NASCAR driver? Her?

But what kind of granddaughter didn't pay her respects? Especially to her namesake?

Hadley inhaled and fussed with the straps of her purse as she slowly approached the entrance.

She'd chosen her funeral clothes with the utmost care and wore a black pencil skirt and a sleeveless black top with a bit of white piping around the half-inch ruffled collar, the strand of pearls and studs she'd received from Nan on her thirteenth birthday, and paired it all with two-inch wedges because, as her mother always said, open-toes and sand just didn't do.

Hadley paused on the sidewalk when her ears picked up the distinct sound of Calypso music.

Surely the music had to be coming from some-where else?

She turned her head, looking up and down the street for some sign of an outdoor band or restaurant. Because Calypso music? For a funeral?

For the first time since she'd left Raleigh, Hadley smiled as a huff of a laugh left her.

Oh, Nan, you didn't!

Mrs. Georgia Hadley Benson had died in her sleep at the youthful age of ninety-two, a spitfire of a woman and the last of the Boardwalk Babes' parents.

During the summers of '58 and '59, Georgia, along with three of her prominent Carolina Cove neighbors and friends, had given birth to a baby girl. One even had a set of twins.

The proud mothers had taken the babes for daily strolls in their prams—and the locals had nicknamed them the Boardwalk Babes—a name used to this day by the now sixty-somethings who'd gone on to have their own children.

All in all, Hadley had four pseudo aunts and ten "cousins," seven female—with the twin Babes each having a set of twins of their own—and three male, ranging in age from Hadley's forty-five to the youngest at thirty-two.

The funeral home's ornate door swung open, and sure enough, Mighty Sparrow blasted from within.

Apparently Nan's last act was to go to heaven with a good old-fashioned beach party. Haddie could only imagine her mother's mortification, and despite her own horror at having to go inside, she smiled at her grandmother's moxie.

She really needed to find her own. Fast.

Hadley stopped as an older man surged through the doors, the smell of Old Spice and cheap cigars drifting to her nose. He tipped an imaginary hat, his triple chins bobbing as he hurried along down the stairs.

The door shut once more, and she paused on the steps, hand gripping the white vinyl railing as though that alone would anchor her in the turbulent storm beyond.

Go in. Sign the book. Sneak out as quickly and quietly as possible.

Maybe they wouldn't even notice?

Yeah, what were the odds of that?

She shoved her shoulder-length hair behind her ear and then just as quickly loosened it when her mother's voice sounded in her head telling her it would deform her ears and she'd have to have them surgically pinned or else look like Dumbo.

Amazing what years of fussing could do to a grown woman, no matter her age.

Cheryl Dummit was all about appearances, though, and Hadley couldn't remember a time when her mother hadn't been put together like a perfectly dressed Barbie and expected Hadley be the same. Even a trip to the beach was expected to be made in full makeup, some kind of flowing coverup that perfectly matched her suit, wedges, floppy hat, and jewelry. All part of portraying the perfect image of a Babe on the beach.

Haddie took another breath and forced herself to climb the remaining steps, heart in her throat as she yanked open the door and forced her foot across the threshold before she could change her mind.

She'd gotten a stress headache on the drive to the coast, and the cloying smell of the many flower arrangements threatened to turn the painful throbbing into a full-blown migraine.

A waiter passed with a tray of champagne, and since she wasn't about to look a gift horse in the mouth, she hastily accepted the offer and turned to face the wall while she gulped it down, all in an attempt to brace herself for the moment her mother and the rest of the Babes realized she'd come alone.

Oh, the horror.

Hadley set the now empty flute aside and lingered in the shadowy corner, taking in the many mourners gathered. Only Nan would or could get by with throwing a party in the very conservative funeral parlor.

But then, Nan and her friends, then the Babes, had pretty much always gotten away with whatever they wanted.

The ladies believed there wasn't much that couldn't be accomplished with a bright smile, a few compliments, and some well-practiced feminine wiles. And if that didn't work, throwing some money at the problem usually did the trick—though was rarely necessary.

One wouldn't think Carolina Cove fancy enough for such an elite group—it wasn't Wrightsville Beach after all—but the families' longevity and reputations carried a lot of clout on the little island. More so when all five of the Babes wed into well-to-do families and thereby increased the status quo up until the last twenty years or so, when tourists began buying up all of the island real estate and muddying the waters, so to speak.

The original boardwalk homes were now owned by the Babes, with Hadley's generation scattered about, away from the Babes' nosy reach. To spy on their kids, the Babes had to really do some digging more often than not.

Yes, this generation left the Babes shaking their motherly heads. Because of their eleven offspring, only *three* had married so far, much to their complete disgruntlement, disbelief, and match-making efforts.

But out of sight didn't equate to out of mind, and the Babes made a point of nosing into their children's lives as often as humanly possible, distance notwithstanding.

Hadley spotted yet another waiter, this one carrying a cheese tray. She really ought to eat something to absorb the bubbly she'd just chugged, but her nerves wouldn't allow it.

Ever since the phone call informing her of Nan's death, Hadley had run the gamut of emotions due to the required trip back to Carolina Cove and the grief that continuously sucked the air from her lungs at random moments.

Maybe she should've made an excuse? Claimed sickness?

I'm sorry, Nan. You know it's not you. My life won't be the same without you.

Hadley spotted the guestbook and slowly moved that way. Pen in hand, she paused. Lah, why did everything about this have to be so difficult?

Pen poised over the paper, she finally signed her name.

Her name, no one else's.

"Haddie? Is that you?"

The feminine voice belonged to Mary Elizabeth —Allie, Sophia, and Isabel's mother.

Allie was the only other Babe offspring who had married, and Hadley wondered how things were going with them. The last time she'd seen Allie, the poor girl looked stressed, but then, what mother didn't?

Smile pinned to her lips, Hadley turned and faced the striking woman. Mary Elizabeth wore black slacks that showcased her slim figure, kitten heels, and a long-sleeved sweater set that mocked the eighty-seven-degree temperature outside. "MeMe, how are you?"

"Oh, honey, how are *you*? I'm so sorry about your nan. Your mama will be thrilled to see you. She's just heartbroken."

"I'm sure." Nan's relationship with her daughter had been as rocky as Hadley's with her mother, proving generational dysfunction was really a thing. What was it with mothers and daughters? Why did they always butt heads?

Hadley's relationship with her own daughter oftentimes proved difficult, more so than with Hadley and her son.

"Where's that handsome husband of yours? Already at the bar? And where are the kids?" Mary Elizabeth asked, looking all around.

The questions brought Hadley back to awareness, and even though she wanted to laugh at the idea of a bar at a funeral, she inhaled and braced herself for the first of many explanations. "The kids started college a few days ago and are over their heads with that, and...Kyle... He... He's the guest lecturer at a surgical convention," she said.

It wasn't a lie. The kids had told her Kyle had been asked to speak at a prestigious banquet and would be out of town all week.

With *her*.

"Oh, Hadley, you're alone? I'm so sorry, hon."

"I'm fine," Hadley said, wishing she had another

glass of champagne if for no other reason than to give her hands something to hold to stop the tremor she was forced to try to hide.

Mary Elizabeth enveloped Hadley in a hug, and she counted backwards in an attempt to maintain her composure. It felt good to be hugged by someone who'd loved her literally her whole life. Too good because the ever-present tears quickly formed and threatened to overflow.

Amazing how such a simple gesture could open up a tidal wave of emotions.

"You're not. But no worries. I'm here for you," Mary Elizabeth said when she finally released Hadley. "Come on. Let's get you something to drink."

Hadley nodded and thanked God for the reprieve even though she knew it would be short-lived. Mary Elizabeth might be satisfied with Hadley's excuses, but when her mother found out Kyle wasn't there?

More questions were coming. The too probing kind.

Hadley smiled when Mary Elizabeth linked their arms and began the slow, ambling shuffle through the throng of guests. The flutes weren't far from reach, and even though she knew she ought to pass given her empty stomach and the one she'd already had, Hadley gratefully accepted a second glass.

"Your mama is in with Ms. Georgia. Come on, I'll walk you."

"Oh, do we have to?" The words slipped out before she could stop them, and she saw Mary Elizabeth's gaze narrow.

"Hadley? Oh, honey, what's wrong?"

Hadley's expression must have given her away. Or maybe it was that, of all the Babes, including her own mother, Haddie was closest to Mary Elizabeth. "Nothing. Sorry, yes, of course, let's go in."

"Wait. Hadley, what is it? What's going on?"

"Nothing. I'm fine, I'm just... It's Nan. I don't... I don't want to think of her that way, I guess. The image. I-I'm okay, though. Really."

Mary Elizabeth's expression made it clear she saw more than Hadley wanted her to.

Hadley wet her lips and tried again. "MeMe, please just... I can't talk about it. Not here. Definitely not now."

Sadness darkened Mary Elizabeth's gaze, but she nodded and mustered a reassuring smile for Hadley.

"I see. Well, today is about Ms. Georgia, so let's focus on her for the time being and leave that talk for later. Shall we?"

Hadley nodded at the question and took a fortifying sip of the bubbly. "Thank you," she said softly, "even though Mama probably won't agree."

"Oh, Cheryl can be trying but we've got her number after all of these years. You leave it to me."

Mary Elizabeth patted Hadley's arm and turned to lead the way through the throng of mourners once more.

Hadley spied her mother at the end of the long receiving line, looking as regal as ever with her hair swept back in an elegant twist, the skirt of her black suit the perfect length.

Hadley felt older than her mother at this stage. Maybe she should've paid more attention to those lectures on proper skin care.

"Haddie, will you be staying in town tonight after the service?"

Hadley's grip on Mary Elizabeth's arm tightened. "No."

"I see. You're worrying me, sweetheart. I feel you trembling, and while I know you're upset over your grandmother's passing, I'm not convinced that's the reason for your distress."

Hadley closed her eyes for a long second before opening them again, staring at the ugly little dots in the carpet beneath her feet. "It's not. Kyle..."

She couldn't say the words aloud. She just couldn't. Even though Mary Elizabeth was the one person Hadley knew she could trust to be supportive.

"I see. I take it your mama will be upset with whatever it is that brought you here alone?" Mary Elizabeth asked.

Hadley struggled to breathe and shifted her gaze to the woman beside her. "Oh, you know Mama."

"Well, just remember, if you need an escape, my house is always open."

An escape. Yeah, she needed an escape. But the sooner she left Carolina Cove, the better.

MARY ELIZABETH SHIPLEY held tight to Hadley's arm, painfully aware of her goddaughter's quivering form.

Across the room, she locked gazes with her husband and gave him a slight shake of her head, indicating her suspicions had been right. She'd told Adam for a while now that she just knew something was wrong where Hadley was concerned. And Hadley showing up to Miss Georgia's funeral alone and quaking in her heels was proof positive something was amiss—not that Mary Elizabeth wanted to be right about this.

"Oh," Hadley said, the word a tearful gasp.

"Your grandmother is still the most beautiful woman in the room," Mary Elizabeth said softly, patting Haddie's hand.

"She is, isn't she?"

The raw emotion in Haddie's voice brought fresh tears to Mary Elizabeth's eyes, and she hurried to blink them back. Ms. Georgia had been such a mainstay in her life, but today was about Hadley and Cheryl's loss, not hers. "Georgia is someone we all hope to embody at her age. Do you know she volunteered at the center and then had lunch with her friends up until the day she passed? Georgia lived, right up until the very end. We can only pray to be so blessed."

Hadley nodded and extracted herself to search in her purse for a tissue.

"Here you go," Mary Elizabeth said, pulling one of the many tissues she'd tucked up her sleeve.

A laugh bubbled out of Hadley's chest at the sight, and Mary Elizabeth smiled at the sound, glad she could offer a bit of amusement at such a time.

"Thank you."

Mary Elizabeth watched as Hadley dabbed at her eyes, and once she'd collected herself, they began their trek toward the front of the line once again. The thick crowd made it difficult to move more than a step or two without someone blocking their way.

Finally they made it and Hadley smiled at her mother and stepped forward to hug her. Standing so close, Mary Elizabeth heard Cheryl whisper, "You're late."

Mary Elizabeth frowned at her best friend, but Cheryl purposely ignored the pointed look to back off and not be so critical. "Hadley's here now. That's all that matters."

"Hadley, it's so good to see you," Mr. DeCamp

said, standing near Cheryl and the next to make his condolences. "Though I hate that it's under these circumstances."

Hadley nodded and greeted the longtime family friend before she took position beside her mother to receive the mourners.

"I wish someone would turn down that ridiculous music," Cheryl said.

"Oh, that's Georgia's favorite." The older woman who'd spoken leaned in to give Hadley a hug before moving on to Cheryl. "Georgia *loved* going on those Caribbean cruises. Told us all about them."

The woman was dressed in nurse's scrubs, and Mary Elizabeth watched as Cheryl practically wrinkled her nose right then and there with the woman looking on. No doubt Cheryl expected everyone to be "funeral" dressed no matter the circumstances rather than prioritizing the fact the woman had undoubtedly waited quite a while before heading to work or coming from a long shift just to pay her respects.

"I'm sure. Thank you for coming," Cheryl managed to say to the woman when it was her turn. She extended her hand despite the woman taking a step forward to hug Cheryl like she had Hadley.

An awkward few seconds passed before the woman shook Cheryl's hand and continued on her way.

Hadley's father walked up and kissed his daughter's cheek before placing a supportive hand at his wife's waist. Mary Elizabeth watched Jerry make the gesture with a tug of pity.

Cheryl was a good person, but she was very set in wanting things to be done her way. Today was a difficult day, one Georgia had made more trying due to her individualistic choices and secret last requests, knowing full well the tizzy they'd send her only daughter into. But that was the type of relationship they'd had. One filled with equal shares of love and quarrels.

Leaving the small family to their duties, Mary Elizabeth turned away and made her way over to the back of the funeral home where the other Babes stood talking.

"How's Cheryl holding up?" Tessa asked, her dangly earrings swinging beneath her short-cropped, salt-and-pepper hair.

"As well as expected, I guess," Mary Elizabeth said.

"Oh, I just noticed Haddie finally arrived," Adaline said, peering over her twin's shoulder. "My. She's lost weight since I saw her last."

Rayna Jo shushed her sister and Adaline shrugged.

"It's the truth. Looking downright peaked if you ask me," she said, still staring.

Mary Elizabeth had noticed the change as well. Not because Hadley had ever been heavy but because her average frame had gotten noticeably thinner. "I think she's as beautiful as always."

"No one's arguing that," Rayna Jo said. "Has she been dieting? I heard people lose a lot on that keto one."

"Or maybe she finally decided to test out Kyle's office equipment?" Tessa said. "Where *is* Kyle, anyway? I've been wanting to talk to him."

"Haven't you had enough lifts and tucks for the time being? You and Cheryl are making the rest of us look bad," Adaline said with a lift of her Botox-less eyebrow.

"I beg your pardon, but who made you the cosmetic police?" Tessa's blinged-out earrings flashed despite the dimmed interior of the funeral home. "Besides, if Hadley can use Kyle's little machines to lose weight, why shouldn't I take advantage of his expertise as well?"

"Don't you mean the family discount?" Adaline muttered loud enough for all to hear.

"No one said she's done any such thing," Mary Elizabeth chided in a low voice, more than ready to come to Hadley's defense.

"True. And let's forget Hadley for a moment. You're going after number four, aren't you?" Adaline said to Tessa. "Before every husband, you run off for a 'retreat' and come back looking ten years younger."

Mary Elizabeth watched as the only single Babe

shrugged and smiled like the cat who'd swallowed the canary.

Tessa wore a dress twenty years too young for her sixty-two-year-old body, but she pulled it off due to the hours of yoga and running she did on a daily basis. But Tessa and Cheryl were also alike in that they had a whole slew of regimes they performed when it came to skin and hair, not to mention surgical, and would die chasing the fountain of youth.

The tallest and thinnest of the group, Tessa had divorced one husband and buried two, with a child to show for each of them. But after four years as a widow, apparently the tide had turned yet again.

"Look out, Carolina Cove," Rayna Jo said, smiling as she lifted her champagne flute.

"Is there a particular someone you have in mind?" Adaline asked.

"Does this have anything to do with you and Bruce?" Mary Elizabeth asked. Bruce Holloway was Tessa's first husband, and the two had been seen hanging out quite a bit lately after Tessa had had a close call with a con artist.

"Perhaps," Tessa said.

"Really? Why the change of heart?" Mary Elizabeth asked.

"Lord knows why any of us would take on a new man at this age," Adaline added.

"Technically he's not new," Tessa said, earning an eye roll from Adaline. "And I had my doubts as well, but he isn't the stranger who came back from Viet Nam. Thank God."

Mary Elizabeth watched how Tessa glanced toward the front of the room, and her expression softened, her gaze saddened.

"Besides, if you really want to know, Ms. Georgia got me thinking. I realized she's been alone the last *thirty* years. If I have another thirty to go, I'd like to spend them with someone special."

Mary Elizabeth managed a smile at her friend's statement. Tessa had suffered more than her share of heartache.

"Well, I say there are no guarantees. You might feel just as lonely as you do right now," Adaline said. "Maybe you should focus on simply widening your social circle and going out with friends more?"

Mary Elizabeth's gaze landed on Rayna Jo before shifting to Adaline. One night not so long ago, Rayna Jo had confided in Mary Elizabeth, sharing her concern that her twin seemed a little too keen on the attention one of their new male clients was doling out. Was Adaline speaking from experience?

"I'm going to go check on the caterers," Rayna Jo said.

"I need a trip to the ladies' room before I go track down Hugh. I'll come with you," Adaline added.

The sisters walked away and Mary Elizabeth felt Tessa studying her.

"Where's Adam?" Tessa asked.

"Hmm? Oh, he was here but had to step out. He'll be back though."

"Business?" Tessa said.

Mary Elizabeth nodded. It seemed Adam worked longer hours now than he had fresh out of law school. But part of the reason was that their wealthy neighbors knew he worked from home a lot and liked the convenience of an attorney capable of handling their business from the convenience of the beach.

"Hey, are you sure you're okay?" Tessa asked.

Mary Elizabeth nodded, her gaze locked on Hadley's strained features. Her goddaughter was miserably unhappy, and Mary Elizabeth's mind whirled with possibilities, none of them pleasant. "I'm fine. Just tired. It's been a long couple of days, hasn't it?" She linked their arms and gently tugged, ready for a distraction herself. "Let's go get some champagne and talk more about Bruce, shall we?"

GRAB YOUR COPY OF SEASHELLS AND WEDDING BELLS, AVAILABLE FOR PRE-ORDER!

BOOKS SET IN CAROLINA COVE

MAKE ME A MATCH SERIES:

- ROMANCE RESET
- RULES OF ENGAGEMENT
- THE MATCHMAKER'S SECRET
- PERFECTLY MISMATCHED
- BY THE BOOK

THE SEASIDE SISTERS SERIES:

- THE LAST GOODBYE
- LATTES AND LULLABYES
- MAP OF DREAMS
- WORTH THE RISK
- LOST LOVE FOUND

COMING SOON!

CAROLINA COVE SERIES:

- SEASCAPES AND VEGAS MISTAKES
- SEASHELLS AND WEDDING BELLS
- SEA GLASS AND SECOND CHANCES

Want to read other books set in my fictional coastal town of Carolina Cove? Check out the excerpt of THE LAST GOODBYE:

Dominic Dunn hit his turn signal and waited for a family of five to cross the sidewalk before he turned into the Carolina Cove Inn lot and parked, dread filling his stomach. Just the sight of the happy families and tourists wandering the sidewalks, lounging on restaurant patios, and enjoying the lively Saturday night left him angry. He should've ignored the letter. Ignored his next-door neighbor and best friend, ignored his boss and coworkers who said he had to honor Lisa's last request and come here.

"Mister? You gonna get out?"

The boy's voice startled Dominic and he turned to see a kid around eight years old watching him. The salt-air breeze blowing through the open windows of his car brought with it the smell of fried foods from the restaurants nearby, and seagulls squawked as they flew overhead.

"Mister?"

"Yeah," Dominic said, only then realizing he'd pulled into a parking place and was literally sitting there with his foot on the brake as he debated his choices of whether to throw the new car in reverse and floor it to get out of Carolina Cove as quickly as possible... or stay the prepaid two weeks Lisa had booked for him before her death.

"Doesn't look like it. Are you drunk?"

A rough-sounding chuckle left his chest. "Do you get a lot of drunk people here?"

"Sometimes."

"I see. Well, I'm not drunk. Just trying to decide if I want to stay here."

"Oh. You got a reservation?"

Did the kid ever stop asking questions? A memory formed, that of his son, Elijah, at the same age. "Yeah, I do."

"Then why don't you wanna stay?"

Dominic glanced at the clock and noted the time. If he left now, he'd add another six hours to his drive from Atlanta. Not how he wanted to spend what was left of the day. Maybe he should spend the night and head back to Atlanta first thing in the morning? "You've convinced me. I guess I will stay."

"I'll show you the way to the office."

"Do your parents know you're out here near the

street? You're awfully young to be wandering about on your own."

The kid's shoulders squared and he lifted his chin to a defiant angle.

"I'm almost ten."

He looked younger, maybe because of his small stature. "Well, almost ten or not, there are a lot of strangers milling around, and it's not safe for kids these days. Are you visiting?" He sounded like an old man talking about "the good old days" but it was true. What kind of parent just let their kid wander the streets in a beach town full of people, some of whom probably waited on the opportunity to grab a kid and head out of town?

"No. I live here. You coming or not?"

The kid had spunk, Dominic had to give him that.

He rolled up the windows of the Porsche 911, killing the powerful engine with another press of a button. He felt a little conspicuous driving the flashy car, but he had to admit he loved the power. Just like Lisa knew he would.

He opened the door and climbed out of the low vehicle, yet another thing to get used to after driving a family-friendly SUV for so many years.

"Wow. You're tall. My mom is too. I hope I'm tall when I grow up."

Dominic locked the car and fell into step behind

the boy. "I see the sign for the office. You can head home if you like."

"No. I need to check in anyway." The kid turned around and walked backward, rolling his eyes in classic kid fashion. "Or my mom will freak out and call the police again."

Again? "Does that happen a lot?"

"Her calling the police or freaking out?"

"Take your pick."

"Yeah."

Yeah to... both? Dom bit back another chuckle. Given the kid's intrepid personality, he probably kept his mom busy.

The kid flipped face-forward and Dom watched as the boy ran up the two steps leading to the office. He yanked open the door.

"Mom! Reservation!"

Dom noted the wide southern porch with its rocking chairs and a few chairs and tables before he followed the kid inside, well able to see why Lisa had liked the inn so much if the porch and office interior were anything by which to judge. It was her style of decorating. Beachy but understated.

The office walls were a soft gray with blue and sand-colored accents. There was a comfortable-looking couch and chair in the waiting area, a rope swing hanging from the ceiling in front of a painted mural of the beach and ocean behind, and on the opposite side, a coffee bar, popcorn machine, and snack area with a couple of parlor-type tables and chairs.

"Mom!"

"Samuel, how many times have I told you? No yelling. Inside voice," a woman stated as she appeared from a hallway behind the chest-high desk.

Dominic stilled, uncomfortable with the stomach-punching fact he found her beautiful. He'd guess her age to be early to mid-thirties, tall like her son said, at around five eight. Her auburn hair was scooped back and held at her nape, but curly tendrils framed her face and highlighted striking eyes that matched the blue of the ocean painting behind the check-in area.

"But, Mom, you have a reservation and sometimes don't hear me."

"A— Oh," she said, locking gazes with Dominic. "Sorry about that. Welcome to Carolina Cove Inn. I'm Ireland Cohen, the manager."

He forced himself to focus on her name rather than her beauty. "Ireland? Like the country?"

"Yes."

"Unusual name."

"Unusual family," she said by way of explanation. She flashed them both a smile. "I hope I didn't keep you waiting too long?"

"Not at all. Samuel kept me company."

"Mom, you should see his cool car! I'll bet it goes really fast. Does it?"

"It does."

"Maybe you'll take me for a ride sometime?"

"*Samuel.*"

"I'm leaving tomorrow."

"Oh."

"And even if he wasn't, Samuel, that's not something you ask our guests. We've talked about this, remember?" the boy's mother said while sliding her son a stern glare.

"Yes, ma'am."

Samuel glanced at Dominic and rolled his eyes, and yet again Dom found himself stifling a chuckle. And wondering at the last time he'd laughed so much in such a short span of time. "Tough break, kid."

"Let's get you checked in. Name?"

"Dominic Dunn."

"Domin—"

His name ended with a gasp and Ireland's eyes filled with tears. She blinked rapidly and managed to keep them from falling, but in that instant, he knew she recognized him—and knew his reason for being there.

KEEP   READING   THE   LAST GOODBYE!

ALSO BY KAY LYONS

MONTANA SECRETS SERIES:

- HEALING HER COWBOY
- IT HAD TO BE YOU
- HERS TO KEEP
- MILLION DOLLAR STANDOFF
- HIS CHRISTMAS WISH
- THEIR SECRET SON

THE SEASIDE SISTERS SERIES:

- THE LAST GOODBYE
- LATTES AND LULLABYES
- MAP OF DREAMS
- WORTH THE RISK
- LOST LOVE FOUND

TAMING THE TULANES SERIES:

- SMALL TOWN SCANDAL
- THEIR SECRET BARGAIN
- CROSSING THE LINE
- THE NANNY'S SECRET
- SOMEONE TO TRUST

THE STONE RIVER SERIES:

- WORTH THE WAIT
- NOT BY SIGHT
- THROUGH THE VALLEY
- LEAD ME NOT
- CHRISTMAS AT HOLLY WOOD
- THEIR CHRISTMAS MIRACLE
- SECOND CHANCES

SMALL TOWN SCANDALS SERIES:

- BRODY'S REDEMPTION
- FALLING FOR HER BOSS
- WITH THIS MAN

SECRET SANTA SERIES:

- SECRET SANTA
- SECRET SANTA II: A CHRISTMAS TO REMEMBER

MAKE ME A MATCH SERIES:

- ROMANCE RESET
- RULES OF ENGAGEMENT
- THE MATCHMAKER'S SECRET
- PERFECTLY MISMATCHED
- BY THE BOOK

COMING SOON!

CAROLINA COVE SERIES:

- SEASCAPES AND VEGAS MISTAKES
- SEASHELLS AND WEDDING BELLS
- SEA GLASS AND SECOND CHANCES

ABOUT THE AUTHOR

Kay Lyons always wanted to be a writer, ever since the age of seven or eight when she copied the pictures out of a Charlie Brown book and rewrote the story because she didn't like the plot. Through the years her stories have changed but one characteristic stayed true— they were all romances. Each and every one of her manuscripts included a love story.

Published in 2005 with Harlequin Enterprises, Kay's first release was a national bestseller. Kay has also been a HOLT Medallion, Book Buyers Best and RITA Award nominee. Look for her most recent novels with Kindred Spirits Publishing.

For more information regarding her work, please visit Kay at the following:

www.kaylyonsauthor.com
@KayLyonsAuthor (Twitter)
Kay Lyons Author (Facebook)
Author_Kay_Lyons (Instagram)
Kay Lyons, Author (Pinterest)
Romance Author Kay (TikTok)
SIGN UP FOR KAY'S NEWSLETTER AND

RECEIVE UPDATES ON NEW RELEASES, CONTESTS, PRE-RELEASE BOOK INFORMATION, EXCLUSIVES AND MORE!

FAQ

FAQ ABOUT CAROLINA COVE:

Is Carolina Cove a real place?

Carolina Cove is purely fictional; however, it is *loosely* based on one of my favorite places—Kure Beach, North Carolina. Kure Beach is home to a wonderful pier, a pavilion for special events like weddings and birthdays, swings facing the Atlantic, pelicans Pete and George, coffee shops, restaurants, and more. It's also close to the North Carolina Aquarium, Carolina Beach, and Wilmington.

Can I stay at the Carolina Cove Inn?

While Carolina Cove and the Carolina Cove Inn are purely fictional, there are plenty of motels and rentals in the area to enjoy. One of my favorites is the Admirals Quarters. If you go, tell them Kay sent you! :)

The pier is real?

Yes! And it has quite a history. Be sure to check out the Kure Beach Pier Cam for a view of Kure Beach and the Atlantic.

What about the restaurants and coffee shops and places you've mentioned in the series?

London's Lattes is based on two of my favorite local coffee shops in Kure Beach and Carolina Beach. Are there more? Yes, plenty. But those two shops I know well because I've visited fairly often while writing these stories. Neither of them on their own was perfect for what I had in mind for London's, however, so I basically combined the two and ta-da! London's Lattes was born. But, no, if you go into either of them, you won't find London's exact business. Isn't fiction wonderful?

Why make up a city? Why not use Kure Beach?

One of the best things about writing fiction is that when a story appears a certain way, you can write it just that way. Carolina Cove and the characters appeared to me in story form and while Kure Beach IS one of my favorite places, I had to change some things to better fit the series as well as steer far away from any real-life persons/families for obvious reasons. Doing so, that meant also changing the name of the city, etc. But, that said, you will find a slew of similarities in the fictional city and the real one. :)

Where is the dream catcher mailbox?

Unfortunately the dream catcher mailbox is pure fiction and an idea taken from a "beach mailbox" I visited once many years ago. The dream catcher mailbox first appeared in the SEASIDE SISTERS SERIES.

Update: I have been told a mailbox has been placed at the southern end of Ft. Fisher but I cannot confirm this.

How did you research the matchmaking aspect?

Oh, the answer to this was fun! Wilmington actually has a professional matchmaker. I interviewed her to get my details straight and learned a lot about a very fascinating business!

MAKE ME A MATCH SERIES:

- ROMANCE RESET
- RULES OF ENGAGEMENT
- THE MATCHMAKER'S SECRET
- PERFECTLY MISMATCHED

- BY THE BOOK

THE SEASIDE SISTERS SERIES:

- THE LAST GOODBYE
- LATTES AND LULLABYES
- MAP OF DREAMS
- WORTH THE RISK
- LOST LOVE FOUND

COMING SOON:

- SEASCAPES AND VEGAS MISTAKES
- SEASHELLS AND WEDDING BELLS
- SEA GLASS AND SECOND CHANCES

Made in the USA
Columbia, SC
20 February 2023

12563094R00187